Doing It:
Five Performing Arts

THIS IS A NEW YORK REVIEW BOOK

PUBLISHED BY THE NEW YORK REVIEW OF BOOKS

DOING IT:
FIVE PERFORMING ARTS

Published in 2001
in the United States of America by
The New York Review of Books
1755 Broadway
New York, NY 10019
www.nybooks.com

Library of Congress Cataloging-in-Publication Data

Doing it: five performing arts / edited by Robert B. Silvers; with contributions by Tom Stoppard ... [et al.].

p. cm.

ISBN 0-940322-75-7

1. Performing arts. I. Silvers, Robert B. II. Stoppard, Tom. III. Title.

PN1584 .D597 2001

791—dc21

00-011545

ISBN 0-940322-75-7

Printed in the United States of America on acid-free paper.

March 2001

Doing It:
Five Performing Arts

by

TOM STOPPARD

CHARLES ROSEN

JONATHAN MILLER

GARRY WILLS

GEOFFREY O'BRIEN

edited by

ROBERT B. SILVERS

NEW YORK REVIEW BOOKS

New York

CONTENTS

PREFACE

MOST OF THESE essays on the performing arts began as talks in a series sponsored by the New York Public Library, and all appeared in *The New York Review*. Somehow the title "Technique and Interpretation in the Performing Arts" crept into the Library's announcements. It was supposed to suggest that the contributors could speak about any aspect of their subject that they wanted to. But for some of the contributors, of course, it gave a splendid chance to say that such words were of no use to them at all. "Doing It" comes much closer. Great thanks to the New York Public Library and to Barbara Epstein, co-editor of *The New York Review of Books*, for making this collection possible.

ROBERT B. SILVERS

The following is based on a talk given at the New York Public Library on March 29, 1999, and was published in The New York Review of Books *of September 23, 1999.*

TOM STOPPARD

Pragmatic Theater

I AM SPEAKING here under the rubric "Technique and Interpretation in the Performing Arts," and if there were ever a title dreamed up to strike me dumb, this one verges on inspiration. It is not that I have any difficulty with the idea of technique. I can see as clearly as anybody that the notion of technique in, say, rock climbing is immediately intelligible. But your actual rock climber, as opposed to a critic of rock climbing, would probably describe what he does as climbing up rocks in the way that seems to make the best sense if you don't want to fall off the rock, and as your actual playwright, rather than a lecturer, I would say that the theater seems to me, on the whole, to be a way of telling stories which are acted out for an audience and which mean pretty much what the audience thinks they mean.

In a while I'll probably drop this *faux naif* persona. I'm not even sure myself to what degree it's a posture. But I don't think of myself as employing a technique distinguishable from common sense and a common understanding of storytelling. The rest is the hard part.

The idea of interpretation is intelligible, also. But we

speak of actors interpreting roles, or directors interpreting authors. I don't think writers are interpretative artists. Recently I was served up as the lunch break at an acting school and the opening question, from a student, was: What was the first thing I expected from an actor in my plays? My answer, "clarity of utterance," got a laugh, a nervous laugh in which I detected reproach. An actor's head is full of subtle and complex objectives, all in the service of the character, and clarity of utterance may seem the least of these—a given, in fact—but it really is the first thing I ask for, and, here and there, the last thing I get. I mean that literally: when the show is ready to go—chock-a-block with technique and interpretation, the final light cues, costume details, and sound effects in the last stages of refinement—authors like myself find themselves begging individual actors to look after this consonant or that vowel. The word "if" at the beginning of a sentence is a favorite for neglect. By the time a play opens I always know how many sentences it contains starting with "if," because they're all in my notebook.

There's a man on the stage and a woman on the stage. The man says, "Would you care for a drink?" The woman says, "Yes, I think I might. I'll have a whisky and soda."

This mildly uninteresting exchange becomes more interesting, more dramatic, depending on the information we have. It's more interesting if she's a member of Alcoholics Anonymous. It's more interesting if we know the man to be a successful poisoner; most interesting of all, perhaps, if we have already seen the man's roommate use the Cutty Sark bottle for a urine sample. Is that technique?

It strikes me now that that's what technique must be: the control of the information that flows from a play to its audience, and in particular the ordering of the information. We interfere with that at our peril, don't we? Actually, no, we don't. I can think of a dozen productions of Shakespeare where the order of information is subverted (it's harder to think of productions where it is respected). I'm thinking now of one of Trevor Nunn's first great successes, his *Comedy of Errors*. The play begins in the city of Ephesus, with the duke explaining for our benefit that Ephesus is the enemy of the city of Syracuse and that anyone from Syracuse found in Ephesus is in for the chop. One of his hearers turns to us with an expression of dismay. He has no lines yet. What he has, however, is a Syracuse T-shirt, and at that instant Nunn's story got itself in front of Shakespeare's.

Directors of Shakespeare do this all the time for fun and profit, and a much weightier example was Richard Eyre's *Hamlet* (again, many years ago), in which the ghost of Hamlet's father was interpreted as a projection of young Hamlet's neurosis, existing only in Hamlet's mind. He conjured up his own ghost scene, the actor speaking both roles in different voices. It may already have occurred to you that this poses a difficulty about the first scene of the play, in which the ghost is present but Hamlet is not. The consequence, or the solution, was that this opening scene was omitted, and the play began with Scene Two, a court scene with a low level of adrenaline. In the real *Hamlet*, the real first scene kicks the play off like a motorbike—short broken lines, fear in the air.

Was that Shakespeare's technique? If so, did he know he had a technique? And does it matter? In truth, we don't like to think of genius employing technique. It almost feels like a contradiction.

There are some who would say that *The Importance of Being Earnest* is the most nearly perfect work of art in English stage comedy. Imagine a scene. We are in the garden of an English country house. There's a man called Jack and a man called Algernon. And there are two young women, one called Cecily and one called Gwendolen. Now into this garden comes a character of whom you have never heard. His name is Grimsby and he is a solicitor in quest of a debt of £700 owed to the Savoy Hotel for food and drink. The scene, as a matter of fact, occupies seventeen pages of typescript.

Years ago, Peter Shaffer said to me, "I've seen the most remarkable thing. It's in the New York Public Library. They've got the original typescript of *The Importance of Being Earnest*, all four acts of it."

The penny didn't drop for a moment. And then of course I remembered that *Importance* is a three-act play. George Alexander, the actor-manager, cut the text down just before rehearsals. Wilde wrote to him, "The scene which you feel is superfluous caused me back-breaking labour, nerve-racking anxiety, and took fully five minutes to write." Wilde was the genius, Alexander was the technician.

There is something alarming about the pragmatism of theater. Turning four acts into three is merely an extraordinary example of a process which plays go through in a commonplace way, just as *Importance* is merely an extraordinary example of the plays which succumb to the process.

For the moment we are just talking about what happens to the text from the moment it is shared out among the people who have to deal with it, and it should be said that in the case of a very few insistent playwrights, nothing happens to it, for better or worse. But the central paradox of theater is that something which starts off complete, as true to itself, as self-contained and as subjective as a sonnet, is then thrown into a kind of spin dryer which is the process of staging the play; and that process is hilariously empirical.

When all's said and done (which, in the case of playwrights, is saying and doing whatever elevates the written word above all other contributions to the whole effect), it turns out that as the play negotiates that final bridge between the rehearsal room and the audience, the difference between success and failure is suddenly in the hands of *real* technicians, people who manipulate dials and switches. If you don't work in the theater you would be surprised by the obsessive concentration on the adjusting of the timing, duration, volume, intensity, color, and speed of a hundred or two hundred production cues.

The paradox I refer to is that the metaphysical experience is at the mercy of the physical event. We go to the theater to "watch" writing and acting, but the responsibility for the emotional payoff in a great deal of modern theater is handed over to the punctuation of very specific technical cues. There are exceptions, some of them celebrated (Nunn's chamber *Macbeth* with Ian McKellan and Judi Dench), but most of the time audiences (and directors) go for the whole shebang, and if the author is present and sitting on the edge of his seat, he's probably worrying about a technical cue which in a minute is going to pay off—or ruin—a page which, months ago, when author and page were alone together, was complete and self-sufficient. "Hilariously," above, seemed just the word.

I want to go back to my remarks about the ordering of information from play to audience. How many of the audience at a Shakespeare play (or at *The Importance of Being Earnest*, or, for that matter, any play which is being revived) are hearing the story for the first time? Sticking to Shakespeare, one might suppose that the audience at a school production is mostly coming fresh to the play; at the National Theatre the proportion would be very much lower. For the next few moments I want to consider only that part of the audience which knows the story before the play begins. For those people "ordering the flow of information" is a meaningless exercise. To bring the point nearer to home, I'm considering for a moment an experience of my own, a revival of my play *The Real Thing*, in which the first scene turns out to have been written by a character (a playwright) who appears in the second scene.

When the play was new, I recall hours of anxious discussion about, in the first place, guarding the surprise, and, in the second place, springing it. It was frustrating—both in London and New York—that we never quite seemed to find the moment when the whole of the audience (over whom we like to assume control) "got it" at the same time. Seventeen years later, in rehearsal again, there seemed to be something absurd about this approach. I had no idea whether the story of the play would already be known to a tenth of the audience, or three tenths, or—on certain nights—nine tenths, but the mathematics were irrelevant: in fact, I realized that my original gambit was itself irrelevant. The whole idea of cunningness, of ambush, of revelation, which seventeen years earlier seemed to be the fun, now was simply boring. I began to think it would be more interesting to tip the audience off from the start.

Following this thought through, I begin to discern that a play which *depends* on keeping its secrets isn't worth seeing twice, so whatever it is that makes it worth seeing twice, it is not, after all, "storytelling" in the way I used the term. I should have known this. I once watched a professional storyteller at work (I could only watch because the language was Iranian) and—as with most of us at most of Shakespeare most of the time—I realized that the "show" was about telling a story which the audience already knew. Indeed, there is something self-limiting about "dénouement" when dénouement is the very point, the only point, rather than the texture of the telling. We can read Damon Runyon ten times over with some pleasure. Can we read O. Henry twice? Or see *The Mousetrap*? When it comes to mystery stories I am with Edmund Wilson—"Who Cares Who Killed Roger Ackroyd?"—and this part of my thesis offers an obverse to technique: namely that whodunits would be more interesting to watch if *Playbill* named the murderer.

Nevertheless, and in the interests of inconsistency, I'm going to argue now that grown-up art is art that withholds information. I am able to perform this somersault thanks to the limitations of vocabulary—the number of concepts we can hold so far exceeds the number of words available for them that certain words—"information" being one of them—have to serve for quite different ideas, and the way I am using "information" now is not to do with the elements of a narrative but, rather, the possible meanings of the narrative. Art which stays news, in Ezra Pound's phrase, is art in which the question "what does it mean?" has no correct answer. Every narrative has, at least, a capacity to suggest a metanarrative, and art that "works" is highly suggestive in this sense, as though the story were really a metaphor for an idea that has to be almost tricked out of hiding into the audience's consciousness.

But *what* idea? There is no correct answer. In *The Fire Raisers* by Max Frisch, someone is burning down buildings in the town. The play is set in the household of a bourgeois family. A sinister lodger insinuates himself into the household. He is joined by a second stranger. They both live upstairs. Periodically they leave the house, and return. Each time, a building burns down.

The household, particularly the father of the household, resists drawing the unwelcome conclusion, even after the two lodgers are found to be stockpiling cans of gasoline in the attic. Finally the sinister lodger comes downstairs and asks for a box of matches. The father gives him the matches, and explains defensively, "Well, if they were the fire raisers, they'd have their own matches, wouldn't they?" Then the house goes up in flames.

Is this a metaphor for Hitler taking over in the 1930s? The author, I'm told, was thinking of the Communist takeover in Eastern Europe in the 1950s. But, to me, his opinion carries no more weight than mine. Or yours, if yours happens to be, "That's how so-and-so stole my business." I say the information is being "withheld" but it's as much a case of there being no (further) information on offer.

I did say that all narratives have some such capacity, but the plays that are important to the advancement of art (as opposed to plays that are merely good in many different ways) are those that suggest this capacity to a very high degree, and—as it happens, as has happened during my time—do so by withholding information in the primary and simple sense of the word.

Three plays which meant a lot to playwrights of my generation when we were young were *Look Back in Anger*, *Waiting for Godot*, and *The Birthday Party*. They are a trio but not a set. Somerset Maugham was shocked by *Look Back in Anger*. The kind of person represented by the play (the representation made for that person by the play) was what shocked, and Maugham had a word for him and his kind: scum. But Osborne's play, though it sang a new song, didn't advance anything deeper. It withheld nothing. It shouldn't be surprising that *Look Back in Anger* was admired by Terence Rattigan (I speak as an admirer, too). After I saw *Look Back in Anger* I started trying to write a play like it, but I stopped because there was no point. It had been done. (It was also true that I couldn't write a play like *Look Back in Anger*, but that's a mere technicality.) The point was I could see what Osborne was up to and how it might be done.

But with *Godot* and *The Birthday Party* the case was entirely different. I couldn't see how it was done. I couldn't see what exactly was done, either. Each play was simultaneously inspiring and baffling. It broke a contract which up to that era had been thought to exist between a play and its audience. There had seemed to be a tacit agreement, up to then, that if you could be bothered to show up to watch something up there, then the thing up there had certain obligations toward you, such as the obligation to give you the minimum information you needed to make sense of the whole.

Waiting for Godot redefined the minimum, for all time, or at least up to the present time. *The Birthday Party*, differently, did the same thing. And although both authors had done this cruel thing to me, I trusted them and, dimly, I knew why I trusted them.

The easiest way to explain why is simply to state that Surrealism, Dada, and that whole family of cruelties from previous generations seemed to me (and still seem) to be intrinsically worthless (though sometimes enlivening, as a fight in a pub might be enlivening), and that *this* was not *that*. It was not irrational. It was not arbitrary. It did not make its effects by dislocating narrative or thought process or the connections between things. "Early Modern" attempts to advance the state of art, in Zurich and Paris, seemed merely childish by comparison. But these new plays were baffling in a different way. The narrative line was pure, so pure that you lost sight of it some of the time, pure as a spider's thread: when it seemed to be broken, a small shift showed it still there. These plays, so unlike Shakespeare, did the thing that makes Shakespeare breathtaking and defines poetry—the simultaneous compression of language and expansion of meaning.

I'm going to finish by reading a speech from a play by James Saunders, *Next Time I'll Sing to You*. I have two motives for this. Firstly, it is a correction to the course I have found myself steering. I think that without a text, and a fairly self-knowing text, theater of the kind I'm involved in is impossible. Theater is indeed a physical event, and the words are not enough without everything else, but everything else is nothing without the words, and in the extravagant complex equation of sound and light, it's certain words in a certain order that—often mysteriously—turn our hearts over.

Look Back in Anger, *Waiting for Godot*, and *The Birthday Party*, for different reasons, stopped me from writing a play of my own. But a little later, in 1962 or 1963, I saw *Next Time I'll Sing to You* and I thought "Yes—that's the one. I think I can do that." I wanted to do that. I didn't and couldn't but the illusion was enough.

So here's a speech, without comment, from *Next Time I'll Sing to You* by James Saunders.

> There lies behind everything, and you can believe this or not as you wish, a certain quality which we may call grief. It's always there, just under the surface, just behind the façade, sometimes very nearly exposed, so that you can dimly see the shape of it as you can see sometimes through the surface of an ornamental pond on a still day, the dark, gross, inhuman outline of a carp gliding slowly past; when you realize suddenly that the carp were always there below the surface, even while the water sparkled in the sunshine, and while you patronized the quaint ducks and the supercilious swans, the carp were down there, unseen. It bides its time, this quality. And if you do catch a glimpse of it, you may pretend not to notice or you may turn suddenly away and romp with your children on the grass, laughing for no reason. The name of this quality is grief.

The following is based on a talk given at the New York Public Library on April 6, 1999, and was published in The New York Review of Books *of October 21, 1999.*

CHARLES ROSEN

On Playing the Piano

1.

ONE OF THE first things a child is taught when learning the piano is to play a C-major scale. We always begin with the simple fingering 1 2 3 1 2 3 4 5, and we are shown how to exploit the special character of the human hand and the mobile thumb by crossing the thumb under the third finger as we play the scale. In other scales (E-flat for example), we cross the thumb even more awkwardly under the fourth finger. This is a basic part of piano technique as it is conceived in conservatories the world over. Nevertheless, it is a mark of the extraordinary variability of approaches to playing the piano that this fundamental practice is not as useful for some pianists as piano teachers think. A pupil of the late Dinu Lipatti, one of the most interesting pianists of this century, told me that Lipatti once remarked: "You know, it has been at least ten years since I last crossed my thumb under the third finger."

I was pleased to hear this, because I too have discovered that this position is in fact very uncomfortable. Perhaps that is because my thumb is relatively short, not even reaching up to the middle joint of my second finger. I therefore find that wiggling my thumb into an awkward position moves the hand into an inconvenient angle and it is better for me to keep my hand at a steady angle and displace the arm quickly to the right when shifting from the third finger to the thumb, and I have learned how to accomplish this legato.

Everything depends, of course, on the shape of the hand, and it must be stressed that there is no type of hand that is more suited to the piano than another. Josef Hofmann, one of the greatest pianists that I have ever heard—certainly the most remarkable in his control of the widest possible range and variety of tone color—had a hand so small that he could reach no more than the eight notes of an octave, and Steinway built him a special piano in which the ivories were slightly narrower so that he could reach a ninth. His friend Sergei Rachmaninoff had a very large hand, as did Rudolf Serkin, and Sviatoslav Richter could not only reach a twelfth but could play the last chord of the Schumann *Toccata* all at once without arpeggiation—an effect that would certainly have astonished the composer. My teacher Moriz Rosenthal, famous for his technique, had a small hand with stubby fingers; Vladimir Horowitz's fingers were exceptionally long, while Robert Casadesus had fingers so thick that he had trouble fitting them in between the black keys. There is no such thing as an ideal pianist's hand.

In addition, there is no agreement on how to hold the hand at the piano: most children are taught to curve their fingers and place the wrist in a middle position, neither too low nor too high, but of course playing rapid parallel octaves generally demands a higher position for wrist and arm. Horowitz played with his fingers stretched flat, and José Iturbi used to hold his wrist below the level of the keyboard.

This variety is the reason that almost all books on how to play the piano are absurd, and that any dogmatic system of teaching technique is pernicious. (Most pianists, in fact, have to work to some extent in late adolescence to undo the effects of their early instruction and find an idiosyncratic method which suits them personally.) Not only the individual shape of the hand counts but even the shape of the entire body. That is why there is no optimum position for sitting at the piano, in spite of what many pedagogues think. Glenn Gould sat close to the floor, while Artur Rubinstein was almost standing up. It may seem paradoxical that some pianists spend more time choosing a chair for a concert than an instrument; the piano technician at the Festival Hall in London told me that the late Shura Cherkassky decided on the piano he wanted in five minutes, but spent twenty minutes trying out different stools.

The height at which one sits does affect the style of performance. It is difficult, for example, when one is sitting very low, to play bursts of virtuoso octaves fortissimo, as with the following famous passage of the Tchaikovsky concerto in B-flat minor:

That is one aspect of piano technique that Glenn Gould, for example, could not deal with. (A recording engineer at CBS Records told me that when Gould recorded Liszt's arrangement of Beethoven's Symphony No. 5, he first recorded some of the virtuoso octaves in the right hand by using both hands and overdubbed the left hand afterward.) Nevertheless, the low seated position enabled Gould to achieve a beautiful technical control of rapid passage-work with different kinds of touch. The way one sits at the keyboard has had an influence on the music that composers write as well as on performance. Ravel also sat very low, for instance, and in his music there are no examples of parallel octaves fortissimo in unison for both hands which are the trademark of so much nineteenth-century virtuosity, particularly the school of Liszt, and which account for the main excitement in the concertos of Tchaikovsky and Rachmaninoff. This Lisztian style of octaves demands a play of the back and shoulder muscles more difficult to manage from a low position. Ravel's *Scarbo*, perhaps the greatest tone poem for piano in the Liszt tradition, contains no parallel octaves of this kind, but only octaves alternating between the hands, equally difficult to play but not requiring a raised position of the arms.

These famous Lisztian octave passages bring up an important point: the performance of music is not only an art, but a form of sport, rather like tennis or fencing. This is particularly true of piano music, although the violinist who wields his bow aggressively like a sword has not been unknown to audiences since the early nineteenth century. The triumphant octave effects are not only the greatest crowd-pleasers (when Horowitz was young, members of the audience sometimes stood on their seats to watch him play the octaves in the first and last movements of the Tchaikovsky concerto); they also require special and painful training similar to the hours of exercise to which athletes must submit. Rubinstein, jealous of Horowitz's glamorous success, remarked sardonically to him, "You have won the octave Olympics."

It is interesting to note, however, that the most painful of all octave passages to execute are not to be found in Tchaikovsky or Rachmaninoff or even in Liszt, not even in the notorious Sixth Hungarian Rhapsody, but in the accompaniment to Schubert's *Erlkönig*. This work must have given trouble even during the composer's lifetime, when the pianos had a much lighter action, since he wrote out a simplified version of this song—simplified for the pianist, that is. It is, however, the brilliant loud octave passages that audiences wait for, just as they wait for the *fouettés* of the Black Swan in the second act of *Swan Lake*, another feat rather more athletic than artistic—although it would be a mistake to deny the dramatic interest of these displays of physical prowess both in piano music and ballet, which have an artistic importance at the very least equivalent to the high-altitude arabesques of the mad Lucia.

The true invention of this kind of octave display—or, at least, the first appearance of a long and relentlessly fortissimo page of unison octaves in both hands—is to be found in the opening movement of

Beethoven's *Emperor* concerto. It marks a revolution in keyboard sonority, but it is slower than the rapid virtuoso octaves of the early and late Romantics and not particularly hard to play.

It was initially with the generation of composers that followed Beethoven that technique first required the performer to experience physical pain, starting with Liszt and minor composers like Thalberg. Schumann does not use octaves like that, at least not at a speed to cause the pianist any discomfort except for a brief passage in the *Humoresk* and a much lighter one in the *Toccata*. Chopin employs them only once and only in the left hand, in the Polonaise in A-flat Major, and he was horrified when he heard a pianist perform this at an unreasonably fast tempo. These famous octaves in the middle section that are popularly thought to represent a cavalry charge are difficult at a rapid speed (at least, one pianist some years ago was rumored to have recorded this piece with her husband playing the left-hand octaves with both hands while she played the right-hand melody).

I have dwelt on this technique, largely outmoded in composition today (the last example that I know in a really fine work is in the final movement of Elliott Carter's piano sonata of 1947, more than half a century ago), not only because of its popularity, but also because the hours of practicing parallel octaves have been conjectured to be the reason for so many pianists' having lost the control of the four and fifth fingers of their right hands in recent times. Béla Bartók in the *Out of Doors* suite made the effect even more athletic by writing parallel ninths. We have seen in our time the equivalent among pianists of the physical injuries experienced by tennis and football players as a result of their professions.

Keyboard performance as a sport as well as an art is already in evidence with the early sonatas of Domenico Scarlatti in the first half of the eighteenth century: here it is the gymnastic aspect of the athletic performance rather than physical endurance and strength that played the principal role, with the astonishing leaps of crossing hands and the rapid repeated notes in guitar effects that were Scarlatti's specialty. With the arrival of the so-called first Viennese style of Haydn and Mozart, there is a loss of virtuosity: only a few concertos of Mozart and one or two piano trios of Haydn have anything remotely to compare with the virtuoso display that we find in Scarlatti and in Bach's organ toccatas and his *Goldberg Variations*.

Late in the century there was more concern for writing for the amateur rather than the professional in order to sell sheet music, although Mozart was unable to please his publishers and accommodate himself satisfactorily to the demand for easy music. It was Beethoven who felt that the desires of the amateur—or even of the average professional—were not worth attending to, except when he wrote an easy piece to make a little extra money. Even then, his idea of an easy piece was likely to deter the average amateur, as with the first movement of opus 79, just as Mozart composed one of his hardest movements (D Major, K. 576) under the mistaken impression that he was producing something that could be negotiated by a beginner or an amateur.

It is important to realize that technical difficulty is often essentially expressive. Composers will frequently write in a detail that sounds difficult but is actually easy to play in order to add sentiment: this is particularly interesting when the difficulty is a mimicry of vocal difficulty—and most of the expression of Western instrumental music is an imitation of vocal technique. Perhaps the most obvious device is the imitation of a singer trying to reach a high note, always an expressive effect. In the Intermezzo in A Major by Brahms, opus 18 no. 2, the leap of a seventh from bar 1 to 2 is made to sound more difficult and therefore more expressive by Brahms through the addition of an arpeggiated tenth:

This mimics the difficulty a singer would have reaching a high note.

These considerations should be sufficient to show that music is not just sound or even significant sound. Pianists do not devote their lives to their instrument simply because they like music: that would not be enough to justify a dreary existence of stuffy airplanes, uncomfortable hotel rooms, and the hours trying to get the local piano technician to adjust the soft pedal. There has to be a genuine love simply of the mechanics and difficulties of playing, a physical need for the contact with the keyboard, a love and a need which may be connected with a love of music but are not by any means totally coincident with it. This inexplicable and almost fetishistic need for physical contact with the combination of metal, wood, and ivory (now often plastic) that make up the dinosaur that the concert piano has become is, indeed, conveyed to the audience and becomes necessarily part of the music, just as the audience imagines that the graceful and passionate gyrations of the conductor are an essential component of musical significance.

This aspect can be abused, we may think: the pianist who looks soulfully at the ceiling to indicate the more spiritual moments of lyricism is a comic figure, and so is the performer who throws his hands into the air to indicate a daredevil recklessness—outdone in unintentional comedy by the pianist who gestures wildly only with his right hand, as if afraid that his left hand will not easily find again its place on the ivories. But these are only excesses. For all of us, music is bodily gesture as well as sound, and its primitive connection with dance is never entirely distilled away.

The relation of the performance of music to sound is complex and ambiguous: this is what makes possible Mark Twain's joke that Wagner is better than he sounds. We need to understand the peculiar nature of the production of piano sonority if we are to elucidate the history of music in Europe and America after 1750. The piano has been the principal tool of composers from that time (less than half a century after its invention) until the present. Piano music is the preeminent field of experimentation.

It has often been noted that when Beethoven struck out on a new path, he began with the piano sonata, then turned to the symphony, and consolidated his experiment with the string quartet. The innovations of the early piano sonatas were carried further in the early symphonies; it was not until he was twenty that he published the string quartets, opus 18. The new turn with the three sonatas for piano, opus 31, was followed by orchestral works: the quartets of opus 59 confirmed the new style. The piano sonatas of opus 106 to 111 mark a radical development, and were succeeded by the Ninth Symphony and the Solemn Mass: quartets were the end of this last change in style.

Most composers, in fact, have followed the same procedure. The first decade of Schumann's composing life was devoted almost entirely to piano music—in any case that is all he saw fit to publish. Debussy's first radical attempts at harmony are found in his piano pieces.

Schoenberg's initial move to atonality is initiated by his Three Pieces for Piano, opus 11, that were followed by the Five Pieces for Orchestra and *Erwartung*. The first attempt at dodecaphonic music is his gavotte from the Suite for Piano, opus 25, and the Variations for Orchestra came soon after. Most striking is the first version of *Le Sacre du Printemps* of Stravinsky, which is for one piano, four hands. He always intended to orchestrate it, of course, but the four-hand version astonishingly does not sound like a piano reduction of an orchestral work but like a piano piece in its own right, brilliantly conceived for the two performers. (When he later orchestrated it, he made several changes.) It is, in my opinion, Stravinsky's finest work for piano. When he finished the piano version, he took it to Debussy, and they read it over together at the piano: at the end Debussy got up and left without a word. I wonder what the sight reading sounded like, and what Debussy actually thought at the time. In any case, in the *Étude pour les agréments* ("for ornaments"), he produced a clear reminiscence of the opening pages of the evocation of the Russian spring night in *Le Sacre*.

2.

Composing at the piano has had a bad press. Berlioz was proud that he could not play the piano, but only the flute, guitar, and tympani: that saved him, he thought, from the terrible influence of keyboard style. The finer composer, it was felt, should be capable of elaborating the work of music solely in his head, and ought not to need the crutch of trying it out at the keyboard. This is an interesting example of the snobbish idealism that wishes to separate body and mind, with the body considered morally inferior to the less material, more ethereal mind. We have here an interesting aesthetic prejudice: the work of music should be conceived not directly in material sound, but as an abstract form. The realization in sound then oddly becomes secondary.

This prejudice against sound has determined a great part of the aesthetics of performance as it is still conceived today. What is considered primary is a set of pitches which we must imagine as independent of any instrumental color: rhythmic indications are less primary (that is, they can be inflected to some extent according to the personal taste of the performer, with rubato and expressive alterations and deformations), but they are still relatively abstract.[1] Any other indications of the composer for dynamics and phrasing may also be arbitrarily altered by the performer if he thinks he has a better idea—they are thought to have less to do with the abstract structure of the composition and more to do with the realization in sound. The directions of the composer for tempo or for the use of the pedal or for fingering are generally treated as simple suggestions that have little or no authority, although both Beethoven and Chopin, for example, indicated

1. In painting, the corresponding prejudice claims that contour is primary and color is secondary. Ingres, for example, insisted that one could not judge a picture without seeing the engraving.

the structure of the phrase by fingering, and the pedal indications and metronome marks were often essential to their conceptions.

Very few pianists pay the slightest attention to Chopin's pedal indications, and most editors have disregarded them, and still today continue to disregard them: they are regularly infringed or discounted even in the new critical edition that comes from Warsaw. Almost no pianist, however, would dream of changing the pitches of one of Beethoven's or Chopin's works (except, of course, when Chopin has provided us with different versions of the same work). The ideas of the composer for the actual realization in sound of his abstract pitches are oddly a secondary matter for most musicians and seem to have very little authority. The followers of the "authenticity" movement have tried to reverse this metaphysical conception, and to make, in an extremely rigid manner, the actual sound the composer would have heard, or might have heard, the primary consideration. They attack the suppleness of the Western tradition with regard to realizing musical sound. We have all forgotten the traditionally lax attitude of a good many periods of Western music with regard to the actual pitch content of a composition, which was much less fixed than we tend to believe.

There may have been a strong moral prejudice against composing at the piano, but such a method of composition has been widely practiced. Haydn always composed at the keyboard. Mozart is traditionally supposed to have composed in his head away from the piano, but in a letter to his father he writes that he is unable to compose at the moment since there is no piano available: "I am now going off to hire a clavier, for until there is one in my room, I cannot live in it, because I have so much to compose and not a minute to be lost."[2] Shortly after Mozart's death, his biographer, Franz Xaver Niemetschek, wrote about him that he "never touched the piano while writing. When he received the libretto for a vocal composition, he went about for some time, concentrating on it until his imagination was fired. Then he proceeded to *work out his ideas at the piano*; and only then did he sit down and write" (my italics).[3] In this account we see the prejudice against using the piano while composing, and yet an acknowledgment of its fundamental utility.

Beethoven was the great figure who composed away from the piano: that was why his increasing deafness made so little difference to his methods of work. Nevertheless, in his case, his genius at improvising at the piano must have allowed him when young to work out many of his ideas directly at the instrument, and he had for the rest of his life a repertoire of improvised phrases and motifs that served him for decades to come. It is also clear that he hammered out many of his ideas at the instrument for a good part of his life. It was, however, his prestige that made composers after him feel guilty if they were unable to compose without the assis-

---

2. Quoted from Robert L. Marshall (August 1, 1781), *Mozart Speaks* (Schirmer Books, 1991), p. 24.

3. *Mozart Speaks*, p. 24.

tance of the piano. Schumann, in particular, felt ashamed of his reliance on the piano for inspiration.

The utility of the piano for composing was its theoretically neutral tone color: in theory (although not in reality) the tone quality of the bass is the same as the treble. In any case, the change in tone color over the whole range of the piano is, or should be, gradual and continuous (there are breaks, of course, when the notes go from one string in the bass to two and then to three). The monochrome piano might be used therefore just for its arrangements of pitches, and the quality of the sound could—absurdly in many cases—be considered secondary.

Keyboard instruments are the only ones capable of realizing and controlling the entire texture of polyphonic music. The use of a keyboard to work out one's compositional inspirations dates from the increasing use of a full score, as opposed to separate parts. Exactly when composers used a full score instead of composing polyphonic vocal music in separate parts is an exceedingly complex question; but it is significant that the publication of full scores took a relatively long time to catch on. I presume that composers used scores as a working device to some extent for a considerable time before the publication of scores became widespread, or even before we have any evidence for it.

In any case, when sophisticated chromatic harmony became fashionable and increasingly sought after in the late Renaissance, the suspicion arose that composers were discovering their effects by accident when strumming a keyboard instrument—a little bit as if "the Lost Chord" of Victorian sentimental poetry were found again. The most outlandish chromatic harmonies of the late sixteenth century are in Gesualdo's madrigals. Alfred Einstein, who claimed that these harmonies induced something like seasickness, thought that Gesualdo must have found the modulations at a keyboard. Einstein seemed to feel that this practice was wicked, perhaps even comparable to Gesualdo's notorious engagement of hired assassins to kill his wife and her lover instead of doing the job honorably himself.

We can find the accusation of composing at the keyboard—which amounts, as I have indicated, to slander, above all when true—much earlier than in the work of a twentieth-century musicologist like Alfred Einstein. During his lifetime Monteverdi was attacked for the same crime; he was said to have discovered his dissonances at the keyboard: it was thought to be sinful above all to work out vocal harmony on the keyboard, principally because instrumental (above all, keyboard) tuning was different from vocal intonation, and the player could not adjust the tuning of the organ in mid-phrase as a singer could inflect the intonation of a note. In his attack on composers like Monteverdi, entitled revealingly *Delle imperfezioni della moderna musica* ("Of the Imperfections of Modern Music"), the conservative critic Artusi in 1600 attacked what he called the harsh dissonances of Monteverdi. They deceive the ear, he claimed:

> These composers... seek only to satisfy the ear and with this aim toil night and day at their instruments to hear the effect which passages so

> made produce; the poor fellows do not perceive that what the instruments tell them is false and that it is one thing to search with voices and instruments for something pertaining to the harmonic faculty, another to arrive at the exact truth by means of reasons seconded by the ear.

We see here the formation of the prejudice against composition arrived at pragmatically by physically testing the sound instead of mentally planning it by logic, rules, and traditional reason and only using the ear in a secondary role to ratify the results arrived at.

It is easy enough to demonstrate that this opposition of body and mind is unrealistic if we consider improvisation. It may not be completely true to say that the fingers of the pianist have a reason of their own that reason knows not of, because improvisation is not exactly unconscious, but it is clear that the fingers develop a partially independent logic which is only afterward ratified by the mind. Perhaps one should add that interpretation, too, works very much like improvisation. In playing a Chopin ballade, an interpretation can be as much an instinctive muscular reaction of the body as a reasoned approach.

That is, in fact, one of the problems of interpretation: a tradition of performance is often a mechanical substitute for thought or inspiration—often a happy substitute, but it becomes a disastrous inhibition when the tradition has degenerated into a lax and unquestioned reminiscence of earlier performance. The unthinking, unplanned performance—and this is an incontrovertible fact of modern concert life—is generally far less spontaneous than one which questions the traditional point of view, in which the performer questions his own instincts. The musician who has surrendered his will to tradition has abandoned the possibility of keeping the tradition alive.

The greatest interaction between keyboard instrument and the process of composition begins with the invention of the pianoforte, the *Hammerklavier*, in the early eighteenth century. Perhaps the first works written with the knowledge that they would be played on the new invention are the two *ricercares* (or fugues) from Bach's *Musical Offering*. The new invention gradually asserted its supremacy over the harpsichord for use in public halls (there had never been any question of employing the clavichord for this purpose): the organ, ideologically as well as physically tied to the Church, lost its dominance with the diminished interest in ecclesiastical music. Even today the organ is irrevocably tainted with religiosity. The importance of the piano was not, however, simply its greater sonority, or even its ability to realize dynamic nuances. It was, I think, above all, the fact that it was the only instrument that could both realize an entire musical score on its own and at the same time call into play all the muscular effort of the body of the performer. A loud note on the organ does not require any extra effort on the part of the performer, and only a minimal increase for the harpsichord (since coupling the manuals to gain more sonority makes the action slightly more resistant).

Trying for a loud sonority on the clavichord only succeeds in knocking it out of tune: it is capable of a most delicate sophistication, and can achieve a lovely vibrato denied to all the other keyboard instruments, but it calls upon very little corporal force, does not engage the muscles, the body, of the performer. With the piano, every increase of sound is felt by the whole body of the pianist, bringing into play back and shoulder muscles. The performer has to cooperate directly in every crescendo and decrescendo: playing the piano is closer to the origin of music in dance than it is with the earlier keyboards that it superseded. The danger of the piano, and its glory, is that the pianist can feel the music with his whole body without having to listen to it.

3.

With the invention of the piano came the structural use not only of a contrast of dynamics but of a gradual transition from one dynamic level to another. This kind of transition existed, of course, before the second half of the eighteenth century, but it was expressive, not structural—within the interior of the phrase, not as a means of articulating the large form.

Only an articulated contrast of dynamic levels played an important role in structure until the 1760s. It is with the gradual crescendo over a full page or more of the score that the piano came fully into its own. Later, with the invention of the steel frame that made possible the large instruments in the nineteenth century, the athletic element of performance became a basic attraction with what might be called the exhilaration of violence. The pianist produces the greatest fortissimo with an exertion that makes him or her feel as if merged with the instrument, participating directly in the creation of the volume of sound like a string or wind player. The size of the piano, however, so much greater than violin or flute, induces the belief that one is dominating the sound from within, like a singer, as if mastering it were to become part of it; and therefore to a greater extent than any other instrumentalist the pianist enters into the full polyphonic texture of the music.

This sense of physically becoming one with the instrument is the origin of the various delusions about the production of a beautiful sonority. If one leaves out for the moment the use of the sustaining pedal, there is nothing one can do with a piano except play louder and softer, faster and slower. A single note on the piano cannot be played more or less beautifully, only more or less forte or piano. In spite of the beliefs of generations of piano teachers, there is no way of pushing down a key more gracefully that will make the slightest difference to the resulting sound. Inside the piano, the elaborate arrangements of joints and springs will only make the hammer hit the strings with greater or lesser force. The graceful or dramatic movements of the arms and wrists of the performer are simply a form of choreography which has no practical effect on the mechanism of the instrument.

There are indeed different kinds of tonal beauty in

piano sound, and each pianist can develop a personal sonority that makes his or her work recognizable, but it does not come from the way any individual sound is produced but from the balance of sound. This balance can be both vertical, as with a chord, and horizontal. The vertical dimension is most easily explained in terms of pure volume of sound. A chord is more or less rich in sonority according to the way one exploits the vibration of the harmonics or the overtones.[4] The pianist must rely on aural experience to decide which notes in a chord to emphasize: the vibrations in equal temperament are not the same as those in a system of natural tuning. In natural tuning, for example, a minor seventh is an important component of the overtones of a note, and the major seventh a remote harmonic. In equal temperament this is reversed.

---

4. In "natural" tuning, the notes of the scale are tuned by the harmonics of a fundamental note. The harmonics, as the OED puts it, are "the secondary or subordinate tones" produced by the "parts of a sonorous body (as a string, reed, column of air in a pipe); usually accompanying the primary or fundamental tone produced by the body as a whole." The principal harmonics of a fundamental tone are those an octave above, plus the twelfth (a transposed fifth), the fifteenth (a transposed octave), and the seventeenth (or transposed third): these are the sounds of a perfect triad. Other higher intervals appear as well. These harmonics determine the sound of an instrument: a clarinet, a flute, and an oboe can all play the same note, but it will sound different because the harmonics have different powers and ratios in the different instruments.

When, however, the scale is divided, as on the piano, into twelve equal semitones (the system called "equal temperament"), all of the notes differ slightly from the natural harmonics—all of the notes on the piano are, in fact, out of tune with nature. In equal temperament, if we go up a series of fifths (the dominant direction, e.g., C, G, D, A, E, B, F-sharp) or down a series of fifths (the subdominant direction, C, F, B-flat, E-flat, A-flat, D-flat, G-flat),

The piano is the only keyboard instrument in which one can grandly vary the effects of the harmonics of a chord at will by balancing the sound in different ways. I remember that when I was eleven years old and started to study with Moriz Rosenthal, I was astonished when I saw him play a chord several times and realized that he could bring out any individual note of that chord and that his way of doing it was invisible. Composers begin to exploit the vibrations of the overtones in keyboard music beginning with the invention of the piano in the early eighteenth century. When the piano became larger in the nineteenth century, this exploitation became more significant with Chopin, Schumann, and Liszt, and the sustaining pedal was used now not as a special effect (as we find in Haydn and still in Beethoven) but as a continuous vibration added to the sound which, with the gradual

---

we reach the same note, since G-flat and F-sharp are the same; not so in natural tuning using the perfect fifths of the harmonics, in which case G-flat and F-sharp will turn out to be slightly different and, indeed, incompatible notes.

Equal temperament is largely imposed by keyboard instruments: any attempt to get the subtle gradations of natural tuning on a piano would end up with a complex keyboard or a double keyboard (double keyboards for this purpose were, in fact, suggested as early as the sixteenth century, but they never caught on). Almost all Western music after 1770, and a great deal of it before that date, is written at least theoretically with equal temperament in mind (although string and wind players can alter the equal temperament for practical expressive purposes). In natural tuning, the dominant and subdominant directions have radically different harmonic meanings and effects. The composers of the late eighteenth century preserved this difference of meaning even within equal temperament, but it was gradually obscured by the hegemony of the new tuning.

development of public concerts, helped it carry in public spaces.

Chopin and Schumann, above all, arranged the accompanying harmonies to make the notes of the melody vibrate. Debussy later created extraordinary effects by this means. A beautiful tone color also depends on an intuition of the harmonic significance, and an adjustment for the graceful resolution of the more expressive harmonies (even rhythm enters into the creation of a beautiful sound in this process). What we generally call banging is simply playing the notes of a chord all equally loud with no attempt to adjust for the individual notes within a chord and the way they resonate. Artur Schnabel's pupils have told me that when he practiced, it was above all to balance the different notes within chords, seeking for a sound that was both singing and expressive.

The vertical beauty of sound—the balance of notes from low to high within a specific harmony—depends to some extent on the horizontal dimension, and the finest pianists make it possible for the listener to trace the expressive movement of the different individual voices within the contrapuntal texture. The glory of the piano is its ability to allow the different voices of the polyphonic structure to interpenetrate each other, shifting the levels from one line to another. The horizontal dimension requires a feeling for the expression latent within the melody and the phrase—and with the bass and inner voices as well. It goes without saying that an accent on a melodic note that sticks out like a sore thumb is immediately felt as ugly. More important is the beauty of sound that comes from recognizing the harmonic meaning within the melody and the curve of its arabesque. In tonal music—at least in what is called the triadic tonality of music from 1600 to 1910—expression is always concentrated in the dissonance. It is the dissonant note within a melody that requires at least a slight emphasis, the resolving consonance a softer release except at an emphatic cadence.

The horizontal dimension of sound production exists when the relation of consonance and dissonance has been weakened, as in dodecaphonic music:

In each bar of this opening of the Minuet from Schoenberg's Suite for Piano op. 25, the last note in the right hand sounds like a graceful resolution of the previous harmony. This mimics the relation between dissonance and consonance, between tension and release, and gives the music its neoclassical expression. Piano music from Chopin through Debussy on to Boulez and Elliott Carter depends heavily on the composer's and the performer's exploitation of the overtones and the ways they act within the phrase.

In the first piece of Brahms's op. 119 no. 1, a series of dissonant ninth and eleventh chords are slowly arpeggiated:

Since the harmony consists here of a piling-up of thirds, one of the most resonant intervals, the chord vibrates more and more as the arpeggiation proceeds. Brahms wanted this piece played very slowly, "every note *ritardando*," to draw out, as he said, its full melancholy. The notes of the piano do not vibrate with each other instantaneously but take a moment for the resonance to come into play: the beauty of the sound depends on the way this vibration is set in motion.

Much of the tonal beauty of the piano depends today upon the pedal, which allows the sympathetic vibrations of the whole instrument to act. Beginning with the 1830s, the almost continuous use of the pedal became the rule in piano playing (although Liszt and his school were more sparing, with a somewhat drier sound). This has had a disastrous effect on the interpretation of Haydn and Beethoven, for whom the pedal was a special effect. Beethoven, in particular, used an alternation of a heavily pedaled sonority as a contrast with dry unpedaled passages.

4.

I have described as mere choreography the gestures that pianists employ in playing, but the choreography has a double practical function. There is the visual effect on the audience which tells the audience what the performer is feeling when the actual sound may be inadequate for that purpose. I do not wish to defend the more extravagant gestures, but I have found that even the most emphatic final cadence will sometimes not convince an audience that the music is finished without some kind of visual indication. Without it, the applause all performers hope for will be late in coming and more tentative than one would like.

The choreography has a purpose for the performer as well, like singing or grunting when performing, and becomes a way of conducting the music or a kind of self-encouragement. Claudio Arrau's habit, for example, of simulating a vibrato with his hand on the more expressive long notes had no effect on the mechanism inside the instrument, but it was a psychological aid to interpretation and perhaps even convinced members of the audience that the note had extra resonance. The graceful gestures keep the performance relaxed, the way jumping up and down before serving loosens a tennis player's muscles. In the case of the pianist, too, the gestures, as I have said, become part of the interpretation.

The traditional construction of the keyboard—its arrangements of black and white keys—has had a largely unrecognized influence on the history of harmony, not completely benign, because of most composers' dependence on the piano for inspiration. The keyboard as it is constituted with its black and white keys was perhaps best fitted for music from 1700 to 1880 and has become more and more awkward since then. Above all in the late eighteenth century, music relied heavily on the transposition of motifs, or even whole sections of a piece, from one tonality to another. Playing a melody in C major feels very different under the hand from playing it in F-sharp major. We are physically in a different realm. Most music of the late 1700s is in tonalities with mainly white keys: as the work of composition progresses we find more and more black keys, and the hand begins to take different positions in order to realize the same phrases.

This means that the center of most large works, where the most important and most distant modulations occur, is different to the ear and to the mind, but in addition the sense of touch perceives the alterations and alienations of the original forms. In the development section of the first movement of Mozart's Concerto for Piano in B-flat Major, K. 595, for example, the main theme appears in the spectacular series of B minor, C major, C minor, E-flat major, E-flat minor, ending in the conventional G minor. Each playing feels physically different for the hand, and we may say that the harmonic structure is immediately perceived by the muscles of the performer. This is the golden classical age of Western piano music, when conception, hearing, and touch all cooperate. The synthesis of tactile, aural, and intellectual experience would be difficult to repeat.

The keyboard instruments imposed equal temperament, which swept throughout the whole field of music, instrumental as well as vocal. It is sometimes said that Bach did not use fully equal temperament, but only some compromise between equal and natural tuning.

However, he transposed his French overture from C minor to B minor (apparently, as Hans Bischoff suggested, to add an H (the German B) to the keys of A B C D E F G in the first two books of his *Keyboard Exercises*). No two tonalities are farther apart in sound than C and B in any tuning other than equal temperament, so either Bach was using equal temperament or he did not much care what the tuning did to his compositions (perhaps B minor sounded agreeably odd and exotic).

In any case, the different tunings had little effect on his procedures of composition. Beethoven, too, implied a system of equal temperament even in his string quartets, although the string players may have adjusted their pitches for expressive reasons, and still do so. He was certainly capable of writing an A-sharp for the cello together with a B-flat for the violin. Theoretically, the equal temperament imposed by the keyboard instruments reigned supreme.

In the end, equal temperament may be said to have destroyed one of the basic elements of classical eighteenth-century triadic tonality—the distinction between modulation in the dominant, or sharp, direction and modulation in the flat, or subdominant, direction. Modulating in the flat direction brings us from the basic C major, for example, eventually to G-flat major, and modulating in the sharp direction brings us to F-sharp major: in natural tuning, these two keys are different, but they are equated by equal temperament. In the long run, equal temperament obliterated the sense of the direction of modulation.

This sense was always present as an important component of the musical system from 1700 to 1800, and it was scrupulously preserved by Beethoven: the dominant was a source of drama, of raised tension, the subdominant a potential source of lyricism. The distinction was already lost for Schumann and irrelevant to Chopin, and an increasing chromaticism based on equal temperament finally drove it out, in spite of Brahms's successful reconstruction of some part of the procedure. The symmetrical complexity of a style both diatonic and chromatic was being eroded by the piano. For more than a half-century, a complex network based on mediant relationships (or modulations by thirds instead of fifths) and on a contrast of major and minor modes was an effective substitute. With Verdi and Wagner, the tonal synthesis of an entire long work is no longer enforced, but the unity of long sections of the operas is clearly realized (and in *Meistersinger* and *Parsifal* one may even speak of the entire opera).

Modern so-called neotonal music, however, is only a hollow simulacrum of either the eighteenth- or nineteenth-century systems. In today's neotonal works, the hierarchical richness and complexity of the eighteenth-century structures have completely disappeared; even the major–minor contrasts of nineteenth-century thought have lost their capacity for controlling the large-scale form. Each single phrase may be tonal in today's new conservative movement, but the tonal structure of an entire piece is either abandoned or given a simplistic form which does not recognize the emotional intensity of full triadic tonality—that required an intensity of listening which most of us are perhaps no longer willing to provide. In Mozart, for example, every harmony is related to the central key, and has a different harmonic significance according to its distance from the center, and the meaning also depends on whether the harmony was reached from the sharp or the flat direction. This was an extraordinarily grand expressive system that depended on a complex hierarchy that has disappeared.

The piano, hero and villain, which helped to confirm the full hierarchical system of tonality and to destroy it from within as well, is itself becoming obsolete. No longer does every middle-class family have a piano, on which the children can pick out tunes and discover a vocation for music.

The following is based on a talk given at the New York Public Library on April 21, 1999, and was published in The New York Review of Books *of May 11, 2000.*

JONATHAN MILLER

Doing Opera

1.

ONE OF THE more amusing hazards of producing opera in Great Britain is the occasional backstage visit of a royal patron. As she makes her way down the awkwardly curtseying line of principals, often more lavishly dressed than the titled visitor, aides and equerries who bring up the rear politely quiz the producer about his job. "Presumably you have to be here every night." "No, not exactly." "Oh really! I thought you had to stand in the wings and tell the singers where to go." "Well, the thing is they know that by the time we open." "I see. Then what is it you producer chaps actually do?" Well, yes, that is the question.

The difficulty is that unless you attend rehearsals day by day, not to mention the many discussions during which the design is worked out, it's quite hard to identify those aspects of a performance for which the producer is responsible. The conductor is visible throughout the show and the audience can see, or more often than not, thinks it can see his contribution to the evening's events. The same goes for the singers. And although he's not present in person, the work of the designer is there to be seen and often applauded before there are any signs of what you might call production. In fact unless the settings and costumes conspicuously depart from tradition, in which case the producer is usually blamed for encouraging such distracting anomalies, it's widely assumed that the design is immaculately conceived before he arrives and that otherwise his work is confined to telling the singers "where to go."

As it is, there was a time, little more than a hundred years ago, when operas, like plays, got themselves on without the help of a producer and there was, as yet, no distinction between the work and how it was put on. The reason is that throughout the eighteenth and much of the nineteenth century a large proportion of the repertoire consisted of works appearing for the first time, and since their staging was unconditionally determined by the theatrical conventions which the composer and librettist would have had in mind when they wrote the work, production as we now think of it wasn't an issue.

The emergence of *mise en scène* as something requiring a credit in the program is associated with the development of a repertoire in which operas with an intermittent history of previous productions began to outnumber new ones, a tendency which has now reached the point where so-called classics fill the season and the presentation of original works is a relatively rare event. I'm not suggesting that this was enough to account for the appearance of an unmistakably *auteur* style. On the contrary, the once-unimaginable policy of reviving operas from the past was well established by the time audiences had occasion to applaud or deplore something which had been "done" to an old favorite. Nevertheless, until operas were given the opportunity of becoming "old favorites," that is to say, until they began to have a recurrent life in the theater, so that there was now a prospect of their being revived in a cultural environment that was recognizably different from the one in which they were first performed, it's difficult to imagine how *regie*, or production, would have got going, let alone assume the controversial importance it now has. Because it's only by outlasting the period for which it was created that a play or an opera runs the risk of being perceived under a different theatrical description.

Depending on the length of time between its initial run and what one could reasonably describe as its first revival, an opera will eventually disclose, or seem to disclose, aspects which would have been invisible and perhaps unintelligible at the time of its première. And if, as in many cases, the original production has already been dismantled and forgotten, there will be an understandable temptation to start from scratch and develop previously unimaginable stage versions.

The traditionalists would argue that this temptation should be resisted at all costs and that the producer should assume the role of a self-effacing restorer, bending his ingenuity, such as it is, to the faithful reproduction of the staging which realized the composer's original intentions. "You wouldn't repaint Piero's *Miracle of the True Cross*, so what gives you the right to vandalize *Rigoletto* by setting it in anything other than Gonzaga Mantua?"

On the face of it this sounds like a reasonable argument and yet the examples are not strictly comparable. In the case of a painting, the artwork is nothing more and nothing less than the unique object bequeathed to posterity by its maker. Additional marks made by anyone other than the artist automatically compromise its autographic identity. But when it comes to plays, operas, or symphonies, where it's impossible to identify the work with any particular artifact, it's difficult to say what, if anything, would count as an act of vandalism. Since it would undoubtedly be an act of vandalism to destroy a painting, and thereby deprive posterity of its continued existence, might one also say that it would be vandalism to conclude the first run of an opera without the guarantee of future performances? After all there is a sense in which an opera ceases to exist after what might be its last performance ever. But not really, because in contrast to a painting, which is irretrievably annihilated when the artwork is destroyed, the score of an opera outlives what might be its last performance, so that there is always the possibility of its being revived at a later date.

Is there any way in which one could vandalize the score then, thereby compromising the identity of its subsequent performances? Someone could deface or otherwise modify the composer's autograph manuscript and that, as J. L. Austin might have said, would be a crying shame, but since there are probably authenticated copies of the original, nothing would be lost apart from the admittedly priceless example of the composer's hand. Because scores and scripts are nothing more than instructions, and as long as a copy legibly reproduces what the original manuscript specified, the fact that it is printed rather than handwritten is neither here nor there.

In that respect the situation is comparable to the reproduction of biological organisms, in which the development of each short-lived organism represents the "performance" of an inherited script. With the death of the organism, a particular performance vanishes forever, but since the genetic instructions are copied and handed on, the possibility of future "performances" is guaranteed. This doesn't mean that each individual is an exact copy of its predecessor and that what August Weissmann called the continuity of the germ plasm implies invariability from one generation to the next. On the contrary, even if one ignores the heritable variations introduced by sexual reproduction, not to mention unsolicited mutations—for neither of which there is any equivalent in the case of scripts or scores—the way in which the inherited instructions are expressed or realized is strongly influenced by the environment.

That is why biologists recognize the distinction between the genotype and the phenotype. The genotype, which is represented in and by the biochemically coded chromosomes, dictates what type of individual will develop, i.e., what species it belongs to. However, the physical circumstances in which development proceeds exerts a significant effect upon the individual expression of these instructions. For example, in certain aquatic plants, the leaves which develop beneath the surface of the water are finely dissected or feathery, whereas the leaves which develop above the surface of the water have a more rounded outline. And yet both sets of leaves inherit the same packet of genetic instructions.

Although this is a helpful analogy, it can't be taken too far because the expression of genetic instructions is a mindless process, whereas the performance of a score or of a script is cognitively mediated. That is to say, it's the result of conscious interpretation on the part of someone for whom the instructions mean something. In which case the traditionalist would insist that the composer's meaning should take precedence and that even if the circumstances are different, the producer has an inescapable duty to honor the original intention. The bother is that it's not all that easy to see how this self-denying principle could be realized.

One method might be as follows. Since the composer was presumably present throughout the rehearsals of his work and was therefore in a position to advise and object, it seems reasonable to assume that the inaugural production captured and expressed most of what he meant, so that the decent thing would be to reproduce this approved prototype as closely as possible. In other words we're talking about reviving an opera by restoring a particular production of it. This is something with which modern opera houses are all too familiar, although not for the reasons I've just described. Let me explain. Apart from mounting brand new productions of operas which have already had previous but now defunct revivals, managements fill out their seasons with frequent revivals of old but still-extant productions. Thus, in any given year, we might have the tenth revival of so-and-so's twenty-year-old production of *Cav* and *Pag*, say, or the third revival of some other producer's version of *La Bohème*, and so on.

Now, with their sets and costumes still in existence, not to mention videotapes of the performances, you'd think it was easy to resuscitate any one of these productions. Well, up to a point. The success of the enterprise depends, to some extent at least, on how much time has passed since the last revival of the production in question. As long as they have been carefully maintained, the set and costumes will look just as they once did, but recovering the performance is another matter altogether. In all probability the cast will have changed in the interim and it would be insulting to ask the new singers to watch the videotape and imitate what their predecessors did. Even if you could persuade them to try, copying what someone else is doing is more complicated than reproducing their movements.

The movements have to be recognized as meaningful, and although this may be self-evident you can never be sure. It needs someone who was there at the time to explain what was meant and what was actually going on. More often than not the original producer who might have explained is otherwise engaged, and the assistant who deputizes for him is not necessarily competent to put the case in his own words. And what's worse, if the assistant is new to the production, he or she is back to square one when it comes to interpreting the helpful recording. The result is that with each subsequent revival the staging drifts further and further away from the prototype.

If this can happen with a relatively recent production, that is to say, one that has been dormant for little more than five years, imagine the difficulty of reinstating the now defunct but supposedly authentic inaugural production. After a hundred years or more, the set and costumes will have vanished without a trace, there never was a videotape, and in all probability there's not even a prompt copy which might have said where the long-dead singers "went" and why they did so.

But even if there were some unachievably magical technique for overcoming these difficulties, so that the inaugural production could be restored in all its pristine authenticity, the chances are that the intended meanings it so eloquently expressed at the time would no longer communicate themselves to a modern audience. Theatrically speaking, the production would seem quaint and antiquated. Oddly enough this doesn't apply to musical restoration. On the contrary, recent efforts to bring back so-called original orchestrations have proved remarkably successful, especially when it comes to the baroque repertoire. After nearly three hundred years of almost silent hibernation the musical performance of Monteverdi's operas has been lovingly restored, and far from sounding quaint, the scores played on original instruments strike an altogether refreshing note. And yet, even for audiences who pay lip service to the notion of conservation, the occasional attempts to reinstate a correspondingly authentic staging of *L'Incoronazione di Poppea*, say, have been much less successful.

However, I suspect that this has something to do with the unfamiliar artificiality of baroque stagecraft, and that when audiences insist upon authenticity, what they are actually expressing is a preference for the picturesque realism exemplified by the traditional though not necessarily authentic staging of nineteenth-century historical operas. Even so, if you are prepared to put up with the initial fuss, it's surprisingly easy to persuade an apparently conservative audience that there's a legitimate alternative to the stagings that they would regard as canonical.

2.

When I joined the English National Opera twenty years ago, the idea of doing *Rigoletto* in anything other than doublet and hose would have been inconceivable, and when I managed to persuade Lord Harewood that a *Godfather* version set in Little Italy would capture Verdi's meanings just as well, there was general consternation among the subscribers. In the event, though, the gamble paid off, and before long this glaringly inauthentic production settled down to become a steady favorite and after at least ten revivals it still plays to packed houses.

A few years later I pitted my efforts against the notorious conservatism of an Italian audience, this time with a production of *Tosca*. As soon as the news leaked out that an upstart English producer was about to transpose the opera into the world of Rossellini's *Open City*, there was an indignant outcry from the local public. We were threatened with mass picketing and the Christian Democrats in the Florence Commune discussed the withdrawal of the municipal subsidy. On opening night, the tension backstage was something I'll always remember. And yet when the curtain came down three hours later, the applause was deafening and the production was revived in the following year without a murmur.

I boastfully include these examples to suggest that the proof of the pudding is in the eating and that the notion of "limits," so often cited by the traditionalists, is more or less meaningless. At the same time, I have to admit that there are productions which undeniably "mess up" the work, not by going too far, but by the clumsy application of what is tendentiously claimed to be a concept. In Germany for example, where I was once warned in all seriousness that without a "concept" I would have "great problematics with my praxis," productions are often disfigured by half-baked political ideas, such as the one I was offered as an explanation for a recent version of *Figaro*. When I asked why the characters wore their eighteenth-century clothes inside out, I was pityingly informed that it symbolized the corruption of pre-revolutionary society and that it was after all the English who had coined the phrase "the seamy side of life."

Although the example I've just cited is self-evidently absurd, it is symptomatic of a misconceived urge to exploit "theory" in the name of relevance. The fact is that one way or another, I have always had "problematics with my praxis," not, as predicted, because I'm reluctant to exploit concepts, but because unless you're a naive traditionalist, there is something inescapably problematic about reviving operas from the distant past. But it's a question of thoughtfulness rather than theory.

Figaro for example is too delicate to bear the weight of a "concept," especially if it encourages the producer to illustrate the corruption of the period or to represent the hero as a sans-culotte *manqué* who knows that his master's days are numbered. As with *The Cherry Orchard*, the characters' blissful ignorance of the forthcoming revolution lends the opera an irresistible autumnal melancholy, which the audience supplies without having to be didactically nudged. And as for the supposedly invidious social relationships, they speak for themselves, as long as the producer has taken the trouble to represent the now well-documented details of domestic life in an aristocratic household.

The questions that interest me may seem trivial, but when you add them all together you have a reasonable chance of creating an intelligible social life, from which the audience is free to infer some political significance. What services does Susanna provide for her mistress? Where would she fetch the water for the Countess's morning toilet? Chardin provides a useful picture of a maid stooping to fill a jug from a large copper cistern. And then there's the room which the Count has so helpfully provided for the newly engaged couple. How would it be furnished apart from the bed mentioned at the beginning? The prompt reply to each of the two bells suggests that Figaro and Susanna will live and sleep where they work, and that in turn means that ironing, needlework, and tailor's dummies will be in evidence, not to mention wig stands and neatly piled changes of bed linen. In other words it's a storeroom and a workshop with precious little space for the *letto matrimoniale*.

And what happens if you introduce the Countess's children? Admittedly they're not explicitly mentioned in the libretto, but at the same time there's nothing to suggest that they don't exist, and since the Countess conceives a child by Cherubino in the third play of Beaumarchais's trilogy, it would be rather odd if she'd failed to produce legitimate offspring. In any case it's a reasonable possibility, and as soon as you allow these unmentioned children, a girl of six, say, and perhaps a baby of six months, something intriguing starts to happen, especially if the two children are ushered in and hustled out during the long introduction to the Countess's second-act aria. We know, for example, that few if any upper-class women suckled their own babies, and since toddlers were taken back to the nursery as soon as they'd paid their respects in the morning, the entrance and exit of these unexpected infants stresses the solitude which gives rise to the memorable lament which follows. It's hardly surprising that, neglected by her husband and denied the comforting intimacy of her own children, the Countess is so friendly with her maid. Who else can she talk to? At the same time, decorum requires Susanna to unquestioningly obey her mistress's peremptory demand for a bandage and a nightcap. Between Figaro and the Count there is a comparably subtle interplay of deference and defiance, all of which demands minute attention to the Goffmanesque rituals of their daily relationship.

Taken one by one, none of these carefully encouraged details would be conspicuous by their absence, but when they are all included, along with many other social observations, the cumulative effect is quite remarkable. Almost effortlessly, the audience gets the uncanny impression of spending one long summer's day in the otherwise unvisitable past.

Although this reticent strategy works quite nicely with an opera set in a world with which the composer and librettist would have been personally acquainted, a work such as *The Magic Flute* requires a more managerial attitude on the part of the producer. For all its magnificent music, the *Flute* can be a tedious theatrical experience, particularly when the Egyptian setting is taken literally. With its deadening solemnities, punctuated by magical high jinks and routine comic shtick, the opera can come across as a priestly prank with a message. You can get some idea of what the traditionalists expect from the question that the management invariably put to the producer who's been invited to stage *The Magic Flute*. "How," they ask, "are you going to bring on the Queen of the Night?" The suggestion that she might walk on is usually met with shocked disbelief. "How can that be? You can't ask someone like that to walk on!" And indeed in traditional productions she enters on something that looks like a Mardi Gras float, as if she's topping the bill in Aztec Night at the Copacabana—a bizarre hybrid of Yma Sumac and Carmen Miranda. That, apparently, is how "someone like that" is expected to get onto the stage.

Now although it would be an exaggeration to suggest that the entry of the Queen of the Night is the key to an acceptable production, it's unarguably true that the way in which she enters depends on the sort of character she's supposed to be, which means, in turn, that the producer has to identify or perhaps stipulate the possible world in which she occurs. The possibilities are somewhat limited by the fact that, as its title implies, the opera requires an unavoidable element of magic. Even so, if one makes a serious effort to visualize what Mozart and Schikaneder might have meant when they went to such lengths to include the Freemasons, the chances are that more significant aspects of the eighteenth-century mind would become visible. At the risk of recommending the usefulness of a "concept," I would suggest that *The Magic Flute* is an opera for which indirect references to the French Revolution might be helpful and indeed legitimate.

In contrast to *Figaro*, which was composed in ignorance of these forthcoming events, *Flute* was written eighteen months after the fall of the Bastille, and since he died before the onset of the Terror, Mozart might have felt, as Wordsworth did, that it was bliss "in that dawn to be alive." In fact, as Jean Starobinski points out, the opposing themes of darkness and light are too frequently repeated to be an accident.* With Sarastro's triumphant declaration that "the rays of the sun have driven away the darkness of night," it's difficult to avoid the conclusion that, in some respects at least, *The Magic Flute* is a millennial work, celebrating the rebirth of humanity under the auspices of Reason and Justice. In which case, the Masonic chorus can shed its implausible Egyptian "drag," and appear instead as the enlightened eighteenth-century gentlemen Mozart and Schikaneder would have known as fellow members of the Viennese Lodge. No need now for that pompous pantomime which opens the second act. The scene is more convincingly realized by re-creating something like John Trumbull's tableau of the signers of the Declaration of Independence.

With these adjustments, the rest of the production starts to fall into place. By representing the Masons as they would have been at the end of the eighteenth century, a production can eliminate the Temple and replace it with a Masonic Library, based on the designs of Ledoux or Boullée. During the overture, Tamino begins to drowse over his occult literature and the serpent, like other monsters bred by the sleep of reason, emerges from his dream.

Now, at last we can reinvent the Queen of the Night, so that she can get onto the stage without wheeled

---

*See *1789, The Emblems of Reason*, translated by Barbara Bray (University Press of Virginia, 1982).

transport. If Sarastro is the Master of an enlightened Lodge, it seems reasonable to represent his opponent in comparably naturalistic terms—as a Catholic monarch of the *ancien régime*, reminiscent of the Empress Maria Theresa, whose raid on the Viennese Lodge may have been the inspiration for the penultimate scene of the opera.

Papageno is another character who would almost certainly benefit from this type of treatment. He is, after all, the epitome of Rousseau's "natural man," so that although he *catches* birds, there's no conceivable reason why he should *look* like one, and once he sheds those wretched feathers, his otherwise insufferable cuteness vanishes, and instead of Tweety-Pie, what we see is an amiable eighteenth-century peasant, happy, by his own admission, to live by eating and drinking. All at once he becomes an intelligible and interesting contrast to the princely figure of Tamino, and we can readily sympathize with his common-sense refusal to obey the vows of silence.

Apart from the fact that it would probably disappoint audiences conditioned to visualize it as a fairy tale, the disadvantage of naturalizing *The Magic Flute* to the extent I just described is that it requires a certain amount of ingenuity to reconcile it with some of the distinctly *unnatural* events that take place in the opera —the serpent, for example, the musically enchanted animals, and of course the unarguably supernatural ordeals of Fire and Water. These episodes, which would be perfectly acceptable in the dateless elsewhen of "once upon a time," seem slightly out of order in the world of the eighteenth-century Enlightenment. This difficulty is easily overcome by bracketing the whole production within a dream, in which, as in a fairy story, anything goes.

When it comes to most of the other works in the standard repertoire, the producer is faced with a different type of problem altogether, though judging by the productions to be seen all too often in the more conservative houses, the difficulty I have in mind is scarcely acknowledged, let alone dealt with. With certain conspicuous exceptions—*La Traviata*, for example—in which the action could have taken place around the time when the opera was written, most of the works in the standard repertoire refer to a previous period, sometimes several centuries earlier, and with the benefit of informed hindsight, or perhaps just the distant vantage point of the early twenty-first century, it becomes increasingly apparent that the events that are represented, and above all the sentiments that are expressed, are completely at odds with what we now know about the bygone world in which they're supposed to occur.

Like the novels of Walter Scott, from which so many of their plots are derived, these operas represent the past in a characteristically nineteenth-century Romantic fashion, so that when they're staged conventionally, the productions tend to resemble the floridly picturesque tableaus of the French *salon*, projecting the *pompier* style of painters such as Hayez and Delaroche. The difficulty is that if, in the understandable effort to avoid such kitsch, the producer commissions more accurate decor, that is to say decor which is historically authentic rather than operatically authentic, the result is not much better, since the appearance of the stage is now conspicuously inconsistent with what sounds like a nineteenth-century melodrama.

One way of dodging this difficulty is to do the work in concert or, as they say, "semi-staged." An opera such as *Il Trovatore*, say, or *La Forza del Destino*, whose claim to the title "historical" is paradoxically compromised by what is fondly supposed to be a realistic production, can often achieve an unexpectedly truthful effect when it's performed in front of the orchestra without costumes or decor, but with the singers allowed a modicum of acting. By the same token, although the paying public never sees it, the final run-through in the rehearsal room is often much more convincing than the lavishly scenic production which appears in front of an audience a few days later on the stage. With the entrances and exits marked out with tape on the floor, and perhaps a few token walls knocked together out of plywood, the action has a forceful intensity soon to be subverted by the spectacular "period" decor which audiences love to applaud as the curtain goes up.

I'm not recommending these as substitutes for fully staged productions, but something valuable is to be learned from such makeshift simplicity. Apart from the fact that it avoids some of the awkward aesthetic contradictions I've already mentioned, the relatively unfurnished *mise en scène* allows the action to sing for itself, and as Peter Brook's productions at the Bouffes du Nord in Paris show again and again, the "empty space" dignifies the performer and restores some sort of mystery to the peculiar art of pretending to be someone else.

Nevertheless, I admit that audiences who pay what they maddeningly refer to as "good money" for their operatic entertainment would probably feel cheated by such austerity, and many of the sponsors, if they hadn't vetoed the production to begin with, would go ape on the first night. In which case there has to be some other way of breathing life into the increasingly effete genre of nineteenth-century historical opera. I'm not seriously suggesting the Marx brothers, though as we know from *A Night at the Opera* they certainly helped to give *Trovatore* a lift. No, I'm referring to the widely exploited and deeply resented technique of "updating." This can take one of two forms, the most controversial of which is straightforward modernization. An opera which now seems quaint and somewhat awkward when staged in the period in which it's supposed to occur can often achieve a remarkable vigor when the action is brought forward to the present day or at least sometime within living memory.

Unlike some of my colleagues, for whom the destination of such impudent time travel is right now or not at all, I prefer to stop several decades short of today, if only to preserve a sense of historical distance or "otherness" comparable to the one unconsciously intended by the composer and his librettist when they *back*dated the action. So, as in the examples I cited earlier, I shifted *Rigoletto* no further than the 1950s and my production of *Tosca* was set ten years earlier. My production of *La Bohème* came to what I regarded as an interesting halt in 1930, carefully based on what now look like "period" photographs of Brassaï, Doisneau, and Kertész. And in order to avoid the touristic Spain of some of the more traditional productions, I packed off *Carmen* for a relatively short journey into the Seville of Cartier-Bresson. *The Mikado*, whose inaugural production is the subject of Mike Leigh's current film *Topsy-Turvy*, survived its loss of Japanese decor and flourished when I transposed it into the Fredonia of *Duck Soup*. I can still recall the incredulous laughter when Eric Idle, playing KoKo, opened the letter from the Mikado and said indignantly, "I can't read this, it's in Japanese!"

There are, of course, many operas whose plots are such that they obstinately resist transposition, especially when they happen to include well-known historical characters such as Anne Boleyn or Mary Stuart. Neither of these Tudor queens "travels" well. Apart from the fact that they are celebrities famously stuck in their own time, there is no way in which they or anyone else could plausibly lose their heads on arrival in the twentieth century.

If these and other anachronisms compromise the credibility of the piece, there is no point in bringing the opera up to date, since one of the purposes of doing so is to reduce the dramatic inconsistencies associated with the traditional setting. In which case, the most prudent policy is to concede the period as indicated, but without representing it in embarrassing detail. In other words, as long as it suggests a world in which monarchs can believably order the execution of their unfaithful wives, the stage picture itself can be quite lean. However, this is a scenic idiom which has to be learned and understood, and as I've already indicated, audiences in some of the more conventional houses consistently misinterpret such reticence and deplore it as something done on the cheap. Witness the objections to Robert Carsen's elegantly spare production of *Eugene Onegin* some years ago at the Met.

Transposition doesn't necessarily mean modernization. There are certain operas in which the drama and music are so insistently reminiscent of the period in which they are composed that when they are reset accordingly, the theatrical effect is equivalent to a homecoming. *Der Rosenkavalier* is just one example. It's not that the eighteenth century is conspicuously misrepresented. On the contrary, Hofmannsthal has conjured up a surprisingly plausible theatrical fiction which compares quite favorably with some of Verdi's sixteenth-century romances. Still, at a distance of almost one hundred years, the Theresian setting seems comically inconsistent with Strauss's waltzing music, and through the increasingly diaphanous veil of its eighteenth-century decor, the world of Musil's Kakania becomes almost distractingly visible. As soon as it's reset in the year that it was written, that is to say just before the onset of the First World War, the opera acquires an ominous wistfulness, so that it's difficult not to hear the Marschallin's first-act aria as a prophetic lament for what one of Strauss's contemporaries suspected were the last days of mankind.

Pelléas and Mélisande is yet another work which benefits from being restored to the period in which it was composed. In contrast to *Der Rosenkavalier*, which seems to flourish quite comfortably in its traditional setting, Debussy's opera is stiffened and disabled when the action is dutifully set in the Middle Ages, as the text indicates. The music has such a striking affinity with the appearance of some of Monet's later paintings, especially the *Bassins de Nymphéas*, that it's irresistibly tempting to try to find a literary counterpart to both. And what could be better than Proust? Apart from the fact that the reminiscent reflections and refractions of *À la recherche du temps perdu* bear a striking formal resemblance both to the music of *Pelléas* and to the paintwork of Monet's lily ponds, Proust's recursive allusions to the ancient nobility of the neighboring Guermantes allow the producer to reconcile the notional Middle Ages of Maeterlinck's play with the fading world of late-nineteenth-century French aristocracy.

In any case, there are dramatic themes in Debussy's opera which have almost exact equivalents in Proust's novel. For example, the disconcerting scene in which Golaud forces his young son, Yniold, to climb on his shoulders and spy on what he suspects to be the adulterous lovemaking of his wife and half-brother bears a striking resemblance to Swann's jealous lurking beneath Odette's lighted window. If the opera is rescued from the reproduction tapestry world of Maeterlinck's Middle Ages, so that the action unfolds in a more recognizable social context, the work becomes much more energetic and intelligible. What's more, it sets up a number of interesting expectations about the psychological consequences of casting a child in such a conflicted role—a question which would scarcely arise in a world in which children were not yet credited with inner lives.

How might this affect the *mise en scène*? Bearing in mind the way in which Proust recalled his own curiosity about what was going on downstairs when he impatiently awaited his mother's good-night kiss, it's not unreasonable to assume—or let's be honest and say stipulate—that having had his prurient curiosity aroused in one scene, Yniold becomes an autonomous voyeur, so that in the production that I recently revived at the Metropolitan Opera, I allow the child to lurk almost but not quite invisibly in a distant corridor so that he inadvertently witnesses the scene in which his father brutally abuses Mélisande for her infidelity.

This in turn allows a much more intelligible staging of the scene that follows immediately—that is to say, the episode in which Yniold tries to rescue a flock of sheep from their forthcoming slaughter. Here is where the device of the dream came to my rescue. Instead of having to do literally what the stage directions seem to suggest, the scene can be much more plausibly represented by having the child sing in his sleep, as he tosses and turns in the grip of a nightmare provoked by the violence he has just witnessed. And I can conclude the scene with a Proustian touch by having Mélisande arrive just in time to comfort her stepchild with a consoling good-night kiss.

The following is based on a talk given at the New York Public Library on February 25, 1999.

GARRY WILLS

Film: The Collaborative Art

THE RESPECTED CUBAN critic Gilberto Perez recently voiced a claim that some would rather not hear: "Film, which sets in motion the photographic look into the actual appearance of things, has been the preeminent art form of the twentieth century as the novel was of the nineteenth." For many, that truth (if it is one) seems to reflect the triumph of commercial appeal over aesthetic depth. They will lament the situation described sixty-four years ago by an even greater critic, Erwin Panofsky: "If all the serious lyrical poets, composers, painters, and sculptors were forced by law to stop their activities, a rather small fraction of the general public would become aware of the fact and a still smaller fraction would seriously regret it. If the same thing were to happen with the movies the social consequences would be catastrophic."[1]

Why should this situation be disturbing to many friends of art? Of course, practically all cultural critics

1. "Style and Medium in the Motion Pictures" (1936), in *Three Essays on Style* (MIT Press, 1995), p. 94.

go to the movies; but for some of them, the very popularity of the movies is their sin, since art is for the discerning few, not for the ignorant many. When one looks to the basis for this objection to film as art (apart from mere snobbism), it generally boils down to one or more of these four complaints: 1. Movies are commercial. 2. They are collaborations, more committee work than the responsibility of a single artist. 3. They are technological products. 4. They mix genres.

1. *Commercial.* According to Evelyn Waugh, the high financial risks of making movies must lead to low artistic aspirations: "A film costs about $2,000,000 [in 1947]. It must please 20,000,000 people. The film industry has accepted the great fallacy of the Century of the Common Man . . . that a thing can have no value for anyone which is not valued by all."[2] But mere cost is not a safe criterion for excellence in art. Panofsky remarks that Shakespeare's sonnets, which cost him nothing but some time, were noncommercial, expressing a private vision unaffected by pressures from his troupe or theatrical audience. His plays, on the other hand, were commercial products involving financial risk for all the shareholders in Burbage's company, and few of us would rather lose the plays than the sonnets. In fact, "if commercial art be defined as all art not primarily produced in order to gratify the creative urge of its maker but primarily intended to meet the require-

---

2. Evelyn Waugh, "Why Hollywood is a Term of Disparagement," *The Essays, Articles and Reviews of Evelyn Waugh*, edited by Donat Gallagher (Little, Brown, 1984), p. 329.

ments of a patron or a buying public, it must be said that non-commercial art is the exception rather than the rule, and a fairly recent and not always felicitous exception at that."

Most commercial art is forgettable or trivial, but so is most noncommercial art. The distinction between good and bad must be drawn along other lines than that of commerce. The commercial forms begin with one advantage which, though it is not always enough, is never negligible—they must strive, at least, for communication with others. As Panofsky wrote, "It is this requirement of communicability that makes commercial art more vital than noncommercial, and therefore potentially much more effective for better or for worse." That is why "the movies are what most other forms of art have ceased to be, not an adornment but a necessity."

2. *Collaborative*. Another objection to the movies' status as art stresses less the social context of their production than the lack of individual autonomy in their creators. A romantic belief in the lone genius as the source of true art is deeply offended by the conditions of moviemaking. Not only does a financial framework constrain everything, one imposed by the capital-raising demands of this expensive form and looking to a return on the investment. Within these confines—policed originally by the studios and now most often by production teams—the writers and director, the director of photography and camera crew, the actors and designers, the editor and soundtrack composer, all jostle for influence, scene by scene. Their artistic visions are often incompatible, to one degree or another, and the result is

frequently dictated by the resources at hand (including the actors, since rarely if ever do those responsible for the film get the cast of their dreams).

This clash of artistic visions could be illustrated endlessly. The Japanese composer Toru Takemitsu told me how he had to fight Akira Kurosawa to get most of the music he wanted into the movie *Ran* (1985). The director liked lush musical effects, to which Takemitsu objected on the basis of the principles and the practices of his own career, as well as his sense that the music in this particular case should run *counter* to visual overload. "At one point," he said, "I asked him why he needed me, when Tchaikovsky is out of copyright."

Luckily, Takemitsu won some (not all) of his battles with Kurosawa, despite the idea that directors should be the sole *auteurs* of their work. In another case, where Bernard Herrmann fought with François Truffaut over proper Hitchcock effects in *The Bride Wore Black* (1968), the musician lost. These kinds of battles affect the making of almost every movie. Paul Schrader described for me the tensions that existed even in what seemed (from the outside) an ideal writer–director partnership, his with Martin Scorsese, tensions which led to a break of ten years before they collaborated again on *Bringing Out the Dead* (1999).

To save the dignity of movies as an art, French critics elaborated the *auteur* theory, by which good work results when a single vision is imposed by a director who bends or seduces others to his will. One of the problems with this theory is that the inventors of it chose examples that were subject to the demands of the studio system at its most exigent and to the patterns of specific genres at a time when they controlled the market. They singled out John Ford, for instance, who chafed under the format of westerns, and who did not edit most of his greatest films at Twentieth Century Fox. The *Cahiers du Cinéma* crowd loved, for instance, *My Darling Clementine* (1946), though producer Daryl Zanuck took that film away from Ford, had another director shoot an extra scene, and cut the film in order to change its continuity and pace.[3] Ford dramatized his independence on the set, but Zanuck was often looking at rushes by night and giving him detailed instructions in private memos. This explodes the myth that Ford shot so sparingly that producers and editors had little choice in what they could use. He was sometimes shooting to Zanuck's specifications.[4]

It is not true that directors are always at their best when freest to express their private vision. Ford was allowed to make a favorite project, *The Long Voyage Home*, right after *The Grapes of Wrath* (both in 1940). The latter, made under Zanuck's tight control, is, in my

---

3. Zanuck to Ford, June 25, 1946: "[*My Darling Clementine*] as a whole in its present state is a disappointment. It does not come up to our anticipations. . . . We face a major and radical cutting job. I also feel that perhaps there may be certain scenes that we will have to rewrite or in some way adjust." Ford Papers, Lilly Library, Indiana University.

4. Of two Ford films that won Oscars, *The Grapes of Wrath* and *How Green Was My Valley*, Zanuck wrote to Ford: "You will recall on both jobs I made a number of radical changes. You provided me with ample film to work with, as you have done in the case of *Clementine*." Ford Papers, Lilly Library, Indiana University.

view, the better of the two. Ford did his own producing to get *The Fugitive* made, between *My Darling Clementine* (1946) and *Fort Apache* (1948). The "commercial" features, where others had a greater share of responsibility, are superior to his *auteur* efforts.

Howard Hawks, another favorite of the auteurists, was not in complete control of his output. The important action sequences in his movies—whether cattle drives or aviation battles or song-and-dance numbers—were shot by second-unit directors. And it was in pursuit of his inner vision, of a permanent Lauren Bacall–type heroine, that he made the disastrous casting decisions that marred later movies like *Hatari!* (1962), *Red Line 7000* (1965), and *El Dorado* (1967).

The best way to appreciate the nature of film is not by trying to evade its conditions of collaboration but by finding in them a specific strength. That is Panofsky's approach:

> It might be said that a film, being called into being by a cooperative effort in which all contributions have the same degree of permanence, is the nearest modern equivalent of a medieval cathedral; the role of the producer corresponding, more or less, to that of the bishop or archbishop; that of the director to that of the architect in chief; that of the scenario writers to that of the scholastic advisers establishing the iconographical program; and that of the actors, cameramen, cutters, sound men, makeup men, and the divers technicians to that

> of those whose work provided the physical entity of the finished product, from the sculptors, glass painters, bronze casters, carpenters, and skilled masons down to the quarry men and woodsmen. And if you speak to any one of these collaborators he will tell you, with perfect bona fides, that his is really the most important job—which is quite true to the extent that it is indispensable.

We might even say that, other things being equal, the greater the film, the more collaborative it is. Woody Allen has an unusual degree of autonomy to make films that express his own range of sensibilities, but he has made no *Citizen Kane*. That movie was directed by a man even more original (not to say eccentric) than Allen, but it is great because he had the creative assistance of Herman Mankiewicz (no matter how one sorts out the writers' roles, Welles never denied that Mankiewicz was important), the responsiveness of a fine team of actors (whose flexibility was developed in the Mercury Theater), and the ministrations of Gregg Toland, a genius of lenses and light. Wells admits that Toland was teaching him how to make movies even as they made the movie. To go by the *Cahiers* people's own criterion of authorship, a personal stamp visible from film to film, Toland is as much the *auteur* in many of his films as are the many directors he worked with.

What happened in *Citizen Kane* is what marks the highest flights of film art—the collaborators goad, guide, and challenge each other to results no one contributor would have been capable of. Over and over we see that a director is better when working with a particular writer (Scorsese with Schrader, Capra with Robert Riskin), or actor (Scorsese with Robert De Niro, Ford with John Wayne), or director of photography (Capra with Joe Walker, Schrader with John Bailey, Oliver Stone with Robert Richardson). One of the reasons the *auteur* theorists liked so many studio-made pictures, despite their attacks on the studio system as stultifying, is that the system was at least a training in teamwork, where people acquired skill at working with each other, covering others' weaknesses, playing up their strengths. That did not supply genius; but it meant that the tools for creative collaboration were there when the afflatus, like lightning, struck.

3. *Technological.* Movies are a product, like a Ford car. That is in itself enough to disqualify them in the eyes of some purists. A kind of artsy-craftsy insistence on the "handmade" as authentic maintains that the immense mechanical and chemical labors that produce film cannot be human in scale, warmth, intimacy. This prejudice is not only expressed against the movies generically, but against each technological advance as it comes along—spoken dialogue, color film, wide screens, digital effects. Evelyn Waugh had company in his grumbling at such changes: "Twenty years ago the silent film was just beginning to develop into a fine art; then talking apparatus set it back to its infancy. Technicolor is the present retarding revolution. Soon no doubt we shall have some trick of third-dimensional projection."

The prejudice against technical dexterity can show up in unexpected places. When I was a judge, during the 1970s, at the Baltimore Film Festival, I voted with John Waters, the Baltimore filmmaker, for a brilliant adaptation of a Flannery O'Connor story, but we were in a minority. The majority of judges decided that this film was too "slick," that it lacked the "authenticity" that can be expressed only by amateurism. Had we been judging a prose or poetry contest, no one would have condemned an entry for being too perfect in its grammar or too knowing in its prosody. But the grammar of filmmaking is somehow treated as extraneous to its meaning. For a moviemaker not to love the possibilities of the camera, the subtleties of lighting, is the equivalent of a painter's not caring for the capacities of pigment or of a sculptor's indifference to the workability of his wood, or stone, or metal.

Art has often depended on technological advances. Greek sculpture took a startling leap forward with the invention of tin-copper alloys and the lost wax technique for hollow-casting the resulting bronze. We have so many mediocre marble statues from Greece and Rome because you cannot melt down a marble statue to make cannon, or breastplates, or bells. The best ancient statues—the most respected and expensive ones, the ones that made the great artists' reputations—were of bronze, and few of these survive. The few that did escape melting, like the Riace statues or the Zeus from Artemisium, were mainly buried, under the earth or in the sea, where they could not be found for ages. These statues were collaborative efforts of the designer, the alloy creator, and the caster, supplemented in many cases by colors added to the surface, ivory and gem eyes put in the sockets, copper eyelashes and lips and nipples, silver teeth, gold hair, and "real" helmets, spears, shields, earrings, necklaces, bracelets.

The most famous Athenian statues prove that we need not confine ourselves to Panofsky's cathedrals for artworks that equal the collaborative labors of a modern movie. Phidias' Warrior Athena, perhaps fifty feet tall and visible from sea with its gilded spear point, took squads of laborers and technicians nine years to cast in bronze sections. The statue's shield alone required special designs from Parrhasios and casting by Mys.[5] Phidias' colossal Virgin Athena employed an even larger production team, since she was constructed to have ivory skin, gold garments, and a huge throne of intricate workmanship.

A project like that has a clear parallel in what I believe is the greatest film ever made, Abel Gance's *Napoleon* (1927), which invented new techniques with almost every scene. The large team Abel Gance worked with for three years had seven principal directors and ten principal cameramen (each with his own separate crew), and was grinding its own lenses, creating its own cameras, experimenting with every conceivable new way of seeing. They mounted cameras on cables, sleds,

5. Carol C. Mattusch, *Greek Bronze Statuary* (Cornell University Press, 1988), pp. 169–172.

trapezes, horses. One was strapped into a harness on an ambulatory cameraman—the forbear of today's Steadicam. They even tried to use a camera in a revolving ball, to give the whirling effect of snowballs flying through the air. Gance became the Napoleon of art, directing this huge logistical effort with visionary intensity.

We should not judge all film technology by the reliance of modern action-adventures on special effects as a substitute for plot and character. *All* cinema is a special effect, carefully lit, cut, and choreographed to visual rhythms. But even special effects in the narrower sense can have great narrative impact when used well. In *Fort Apache* (1948), Ford makes his characters in one scene move through a cloud of ambiguity kicked up by the dust from Indians' horses. When the actual dust refused to go or to stay where Ford wanted it, he supplemented it with smoke, and had his cinematographer, Archie Stout, use special lenses and film to give the amalgam of dust and smoke a mysterious silkiness. The tricks are not noticeable by the ordinary viewer. Many of the best special effects are ones the audience is unaware of—like a subtle slowing of motion to emphasize the importance of an incident. When Oliver Stone was watching *Platoon* some years after making it, even he could not remember which effects were digitally enhanced.

4. *Mixed genres*. A movie combines drama, photography, choreography, and music, making it one of the "bastard arts," like opera and ballet, that can be accused of seeming less than the sum of their parts.

Opera has been dismissed by some as program music, neither as profound as pure music nor as gripping as unaccompanied drama. But opera can do what other forms of drama cannot—make time elastic, for instance, as a love duet goes inward rather than forward to explore realms of emotion as time "stands still." It can do what pure music does not, as when the exploration of an inward time is united with a diachronic forward drive of plot: even while complex personal relationships are being explored in the Act II quartet of Verdi's *Otello*, Iago is spinning his web, capturing the handkerchief that will doom his lord. And ballet can make the body a symbol of the soul, freed or bound, inspired or tortured. But movies can do to time all that opera does, and they can do more to space than ballet does.

Ballet can use the stage inventively, shifting scenery even while the dance continues. But the scenery, like the dancers, moves within the allotted space, not out of it. Early Douglas Fairbanks movies are essentially ballets, in which he dances over spaces opened up beyond any fixed stage's possibilities. Yet film can also invent a new kind of space—spiritual space. In *The Black Pirate* (1926), when his pirate band rescues Fairbanks from the hold of a ship where he is besieged by swordsmen, they lift him in a fluid action, passing him from hand to hand in a steady rising motion through level after level of the ship till he reaches the upper deck. The camera follows this ascent, keeping pace with it, by looking "through" the sides of the ship. It is a powerful enactment of the meaning of leadership, of the leader's necessary reliance on followers, who lift him in a secular resurrection, one that breaks through physical barriers with emotional energy.

There is a similar use of space to convey the essence of leadership—one that no play could achieve on the stage—in Gance's *Napoleon.* Riding in a carriage to take over his troops in Italy, Napoleon is impatient to be at the front. He takes the horse of a guard conducting his carriage and rides ahead alone, coming toward us at top speed past the logistical line of supplies that is being moved more slowly to the Alps. This is one of those points where Gance opens up the action to cover three juxtaposed screens. Napoleon's ride is flashed on both side screens, but in the middle one we see the people's army marching toward us with a song. These scenes in combination tell us that Napoleon cannot fly on his own, that his speed depends on the solid motion of the people, who supply a kind of ground bass to his obbligato virtuosity.

In another episode, Gance first juxtaposes two different spaces, then superimposes one on the other. Fleeing from Corsica in a small boat, Napoleon wrestles with a storm at sea, one that tears at the tricolor flag he is using as a sail. Intercut into this storm are scenes of the National Assembly in turmoil, human waves of passion lashed high by opposed views on the Terror. After cutting back and forth between these images, Gance then conflates them, forecasting Napoleon's power to impose his will on human as well as natural disorder.

Other superimpositions give us Napoleon's way of seeing the world. When he looks at a giant globe, for instance, yearning to dominate it, he sees Josephine's face mirrored on its curving surface, a quick and vivid glimpse of the erotics of power. In an earlier passage, showing us Napoleon as a child, schoolmates have released the boy's pet eagle. The child is sobbing in a loft when the eagle returns to him unbeckoned. Later, when Napoleon turns his head to scan the horizon, we see the eagle's head superimposed on his features—a vision of power, but also a reminder of the hurt child that is connected with the eagle's appearance. Gance creates layers of meaning visually.

Most cinematic uses of space enlarge the action. Gance can also use space to shrink his actor. In a later scene of the National Assembly hall, we look down on a dark and empty space that was earlier filled with crowds in conflict. Below us, to the side, a tiny door opens, and Napoleon stands there, a lonely silhouette in the rectangle of light. After he advances to the rostrum and looks out from it, ghosts people the hall, fallen giants of the Revolution's early days, threatening their curse if he betrays their hopes—a foreshadowing of the films Gance meant to make showing how Napoleon deserted the Revolution. (Only the fact that Gance could not raise money to complete his series makes people think he is an unconflicted celebrant of Napoleon's genius.)

Film's treatment of space is equaled by its power to shift time about, to slow or speed it up, to juxtapose different times by flashback, flash-forward, or flash-across, each sequence moving at its own pace. This time travel can be unified or disjoined by music, which puts another layer of temporal measure on the action. Eisenstein's savage treatment of the knightly religious order in *Alexander Nevsky* (1938) would not bite as deep without Prokofiev's caricature of Latin chant. Under the dazzling display of Yukio Mishima's alternate identities in Paul Schrader's *Mishima* (1985), the inevitability of the protagonist's fated character is underlined by Philip Glass's score—which Scorsese admired so much that he went to Glass for the music to his own Asian drama, *Kundun* (1998). For Scorsese's earlier film *The Last Temptation of Christ* (1988), Peter Gabriel found the exotic musical instruments that would convey the movie's ascetic weirdness.

Toru Takemitsu liked to use music to undermine rather than underline what the eye was seeing, playing "off the beat" of the action, contrasting pure music with coarse images and vice versa. Most composers tailor their work to the editor's version of a film, but Takemitsu collaborated with his directors, and persuaded Masahiro Shinoda to cut the images to fit the music in *Double Suicide* (1969).[6]

The collaborative aspect of film has assembled great pools of talent for the writing, designing, lighting, filming, directing, acting, and editing of movies—a concentration of effort that does reach the level of Panofsky's comparison with the cathedral projects of the high Middle Ages. The always-new technical potential of

---

6. *Toru Takemitsu*, a documentary directed by Charlotte Zwerin, is available in the Sony Music for the Movies series, 1995.

film keeps these talents on the stretch. Fifty years from now, many of the movies being made today will still be watched. Not anywhere near as many of this year's novels will still be read then. When Robert Hughes ended his 1997 survey of American art, *American Visions*, with a general lament for the decline of creativity, he was able to indulge his good-old-days-ism only because he did not take film seriously as an art. It is not a mistake that our descendants will make when they look back on our era.

"Burt Bacharach Comes Back" was first published in The New York Review of Books *of May 6, 1999, as a review of* The Look of Love: The Burt Bacharach Collection, *a compilation produced by Patrick Milligan on three compact discs (Rhino 75339-2), and of* Great Jewish Music: Burt Bacharach, *produced by John Zorn, on two compact discs (Tzadik TZ7114-2).*

GEOFFREY O'BRIEN

Burt Bacharach Comes Back

1.

THIS IS WHAT a cultural resurrection looks like nowadays when the system is really working. The machinery is oiled and the gears properly lined up as a body of once-discarded material is inserted again and permitted to work its way, at first randomly (as a test) and then with increasing calculation, through the layers of the marketing universe, to issue as a collection of shrink-wrapped products to be duly catalogued and appraised in a range of magazines and television shows.

The case in point is that of the music of Burt Bacharach, the songwriter, film composer, arranger, and producer (and sometime performer) who enjoyed a remarkable run of hit records throughout the 1960s and then largely disappeared from view, after a disastrous 1973 musical version of *Lost Horizon* and the breakup of his long collaboration with the lyricist Hal David. In the twelve years or so of unbroken success preceding the Shangri-La debacle, he had come to be viewed not only as a last bastion of the Tin Pan Alley tradition of the well-crafted song—hitting the Top 40 again and again with songs that even Tony Bennett could love—but as an involuntary emblem of whatever notion of luxurious glamour the beleaguered epoch could cling to. If discussions of his music tended to revolve around the complexity of its meters or the novelty of its instrumentation, discussions of Bacharach himself focused on things like his marriage (one of four) in 1965 to Angie Dickinson, the casual elegance of his clothes, the relaxed, almost bashful grace with which he appeared to enjoy the comfortable trappings of his life, his movie-star looks (he was, in the words of Sammy Cahn, "the only songwriter who doesn't look like a dentist").

The brilliance of his music seemed to bestow on him the rare fate of being able to enjoy his good fortune without the slightest twinge of guilt: he was simply the luckiest of guys. Then, having achieved this apotheosis, he proceeded to fade slowly into a Southern Californian haze. Not that he ever stopped working, or indeed altogether stopped having hits; he won an Oscar for the main title theme from the 1981 movie *Arthur*; he married the songwriter Carole Bayer Sager and collaborated with her extensively; with Sager and a number of others he wrote the 1985 song "That's What Friends Are For," whose profits were donated to help fund AIDS research. These however were little more than afterechoes of the stream of songs he wrote for Dionne Warwick and other singers during the period that generated now-standard tunes such as "Wives and Lovers" (1963), "Walk On By" (1964), "What the World Needs Now Is Love" (1965), "Alfie," and "I Say a Little Prayer" (both 1967), to cite only some of those that have been most hackneyed through repetition.

Perhaps the worst enemy of Bacharach's reputation was the numbing effect of hearing his five or six most familiar songs trotted out on oldies stations or transmuted into appropriate background music for the waiting room at the clinic or the lull before the in-flight movie starts. After a decade or so of "Do You Know the Way to San Jose," its once-novel melody seemed no more adventurous a prospect than a promenade on a treadmill. It became difficult to hear the orchestral textures and structural intricacies that had once made Bacharach's music seem an exploration of interesting and unknown territory. Far from being an emblem of what was most exciting about popular music in the 1960s, Bacharach was on his way to becoming a symbol of the sort of scientifically crafted, antiseptically perfect romantic balladry that ends up being sold as fodder for nostalgia to insomniacs—"this collection is not available in stores"—on late-night television.

Bacharach's reemergence became noticeable when younger musicians such as Elvis Costello, Eric Matthews, the Cranberries, Oasis, Yo La Tengo, Stereolab, and the Pizzicato Five began to pay tribute through "cover versions" (reinterpretations), imitations, and allusions, or gave interviews making much of Bacharach's influence on their work. The revamping, or more precisely reversal, of Bacharach's reputation evolved further under the guidance of the composer John Zorn, who oversaw performances of Bacharach's music (newly arranged or disarranged) at the Knitting Factory and elsewhere by a variety of downtown New York avant-gardists inspired by what Zorn described as "advanced harmonies and chord changes with unexpected turnarounds and modulations, unusual changing time signatures and rhythmic twists, often in uneven numbers of bars." This extended project culminated in a number of concerts uptown at the Kaufman Cultural Center in 1997, and the simultaneous release (under the provocatively puzzling rubric of *Great Jewish Music*) of a double-CD set featuring such postmodern all-arounders as the guitarist Marc Ribot, the trumpet player Dave Douglas, and the cellist Erik Friedlander.

While such approval bestowed a kind of hipness by association, a more mainstream recycling was achieved through the interpolation of Bacharach's old songs into the soundtracks of movies such as *The First Wives Club*, *My Best Friend's Wedding*, and *Romy and Michele's High School Reunion*. Since movie soundtracks now are often simply compilations of preexisting recordings, they serve to introduce younger audiences to the hits of previous generations, a purpose once served by television variety shows of a sort that no longer exists. The expanding Internet, in the meantime, revealed an international corps of Bacharach aficionados, Nils of Sweden and Roberto of Italy and Ian of Australia and the fan who declared "I am Japanese Bacharachmania," tirelessly swapping factoids and lists of favorite songs. The revival had gathered sufficient steam by 1997 to prompt a campy guest appearance in the retro-Sixties comedy *Austin Powers*, in which Bacharach came dangerously close to figuring as a sort of Liberace of the Pop Art era.

Bacharach naturally participated in the revival, staging a highly successful tour with the singer of his greatest hits, Dionne Warwick, with whom he also appeared on a luxurious New Year's Eve special calculated to suggest the return of an elegance lost since, say, Guy Lombardo and His Royal Canadians; collaborating successfully with Elvis Costello on the song "God Give Me Strength" (from the movie *Grace of My Heart*), and following it up with *Painted From Memory*, a heavily promoted album of new songs co-written with Costello. (The album turned out to be something of a return to form, despite the limitations of Costello's singing.) Another television special, "One Amazing Night," featured Bacharach in company with contemporary stars such as Sheryl Crow, All Saints, and Barenaked Ladies, and was subsequently released in CD and video form. In the meantime, a flood of CD reissues of earlier recordings has culminated in an ambitious box set from Rhino (*The Look of Love: The Burt Bacharach Collection*) which surveys Bacharach's progress in the years since his first hit, the 1957 Marty Robbins record "The Story of My Life."

In such a process, the myth of the original career is amplified by the myth of the return, each step of the comeback charted as part of a legendary progression: years of glory, years in limbo, years of triumphant rebirth. The past is symbolically brought into the present, so that through the contemplation of Bacharach and his music—not as museum exhibit but as living presence—latter-day devotees can gain access to a realm of lost bliss. By a back-derivation typical of pop revivals, the fantasy glamour of the original songs is translated into a description of the era in which they originated, as if life in the early Sixties had been a live-action Dionne Warwick song, with deft periodic accentuation by oboe, xylophone, or celeste. For those who were there the first time around—including those of us who were Bacharach enthusiasts, for whom, before *Pet Sounds* or *Revolver*, the 1964 Kapp release *Burt Bacharach—Hit Maker!* was the cult album of choice—it all has the predictable eeriness of seeing experience transmuted into its movie-of-the-week version, as one moment's dawning sensibility becomes another's irresistible marketing opportunity.

Bacharach of course always had as many detractors as admirers. That Rhino's new box set has been received with contempt in some quarters—Robert Christgau in *The Village Voice* spoke of "fancy hackwork," while Neil Strauss of *The New York Times* announced that "the Burt Bacharach revival stops here"—may reflect an ancient antipathy among those who preferred their rock-and-roll untainted by association with string sections, nightclubs, television specials, or the likes of such "plastic" middle-of-the-road pop singers as Tony Orlando, Tom Jones, or the Carpenters. On the other hand, as the critic Francis Davis observed in a remarkable essay on the history of Bacharach's reputation, "he is a cultural signifier...pressed into service by pop-record reviewers to commend groups that at least recognize the value of good songs, even if they haven't figured out how to write any yet."[1] Bacharach was often enough invoked in the Sixties as a rejoinder to the musically illiterate, virtually as a remnant of higher culture holding his own against the onslaught of untutored garage bands. The singer Anthony Newley was quoted to that effect on the back of *Hit Maker!*[2]: "Burt Bacharach has revolutionized the world of commercial recording in the most unlikely way—he has replaced noise with creative music."

In the event, Bacharach's revolution was to be drowned out by layers of noise that would have been unimaginable to Newley, who presumably was reacting against nothing more threatening to his sense of musical decorum than the Rolling Stones' "I Wanna Be Your Man" or perhaps "Surfin' Bird," by the Trashmen, instead of anticipating further decades of psychedelic jams, heavy metal three-chord anthems, punk abrasions, and rumbling chasms of trance-inducing amplified bass patterns.

2.

The question remains how much the renewed appeal of Bacharach's work owes to the fortuitous kitschiness of the associations it can evoke, to what extent he

---

1. Francis Davis, "The Man from Heaven," *Atlantic Monthly*, June 1997.

2. *Hit Maker!* has recently been reissued under the title *Burt Bacharach Plays His Hits*, by MCA Records (MCAD-11681).

endures as an artifact of the martini-and-cigar subculture, a mere strand in the gaudy tapestry of Lounge: the music track for a lost dream of adulthood set in an alternative Kennedy Era, in which the man who reads *Playboy* meets the *Cosmopolitan* girl on a spring evening in Central Park and discovers that Romance really exists.

The wider backdrop to Bacharach's comeback was the lounge music revival, a phenomenon involving the recycling of Hawaiian exotica and spy movie soundtracks, surf instrumentals, bachelor-pad classics of the stereophonic revolution by easy-listening maestros such as Juan Garcia Esquivel and Ferrante & Teicher, bouncy main title themes from Italian sex comedies, "smooth jazz" (as the current nomenclature has it) in the manner of the vibraphonist Cal Tjader and the pianist Vince Guaraldi, big-band adaptations of pop tunes and TV detective themes, the back catalogs of forgotten torch singers and second-tier nightclub crooners, perhaps at the outer limit Dean Martin singing Christmas favorites: a permissive range extending almost (but not quite) as far as garage-sale standbys like André Kostelanetz and Mantovani.

Permissiveness is the key here. The listener is encouraged to surrender to music that not so long ago might have been defined as the Other, the enemy, the counter-counterculture, but at the same time he is left free to distort or reimagine it in any way that suits. History in this sense amounts to little more than a crowded closet from which, with a bit of scrounging, useable bits of fabric or costume jewelry can be salvaged.

"Lounge music" is a deliberately unhistorical term designed to allow customers to recombine disparate bits of the past into whatever musical world they want. A capacious reference book, *MusicHound Lounge: The Essential Album Guide to Martini Music and Easy Listening*,[3] proposes a category encompassing Coleman Hawkins, Gordon Lightfoot, Nino Rota, The Four Preps, Jimmy Durante, Tito Puente, Carmen McRae, the 101 Strings, the Swingle Singers, Erik Satie, and Rodgers and Hart, not to mention the good-for-a-laugh albums released by such "singers" as Leonard Nimoy and Robert Mitchum. (No one has yet reissued the album where Yvette Mimieux read the poetry of Baudelaire accompanied by Ali Akhbar Khan on sarod, but the moment cannot be too far distant.) "Lounge music" has a definition whose purpose is to undermine the notion of definition as such, appropriately for a mix'n'-match music cobbled out of any elements that grab you: Marimba? Theremin? Bossa nova beat? Cheesy echo effects? Hammond organ? Surf guitar? Close harmony background singers? Mariachi trumpet? Cowbells? Tuned bongos? Wind chimes? Press the buttons for the fantasy combo of your choice and a mix tape will be generated automatically.

Partly lounge music represents a generational shift conspiring to admit a range of musical effects that rock had excluded in order to preserve the purity of its

---

3. Edited by Steve Knopper (Visible Ink, 1998). The field has also been surveyed in Dylan Jones, *Ultra Lounge: The Lexicon of Easy Listening* (Universe/St. Martin's, 1997).

identity. If one posits (as a worst-case scenario) a sonic consciousness restricted to heavy metal, punk, and grunge, and then imagines the sudden infusion of, say, the instrumental "exotica" of the bandleader Martin Denny, it becomes possible to grasp the revolutionary possibilities of tracks like "Stone God" or "Jungle River Boat." A new sensuous universe opens. Glissandos, bird calls, the undulation of waves and steel guitars: the massage music works its way into pressure points that grunge had failed to reach. Irony quickly becomes a dead issue: finally you are left alone with your ears. Either you get pleasure from listening to Martin Denny or the Hollyridge Strings, or you don't; the only variations are on the order of how much pleasure, repeated how many times. Irony meets its double, banality, as the alienated contemplation of schmaltz merges with the unrepentant enjoyment of it; or doesn't quite merge, the mind clinging to a detachment in which unironic enjoyment is almost successfully simulated. You get all the pleasurable abandon of sincerity with none of the heartbreak.

There is a certain appropriateness in the soundtrack of *fin de siècle* America shaping up as a potpourri of decades-old mood music, movie music, elevator-and-supermarket music. Having long since got used to hearing canned versions of Bob Marley and Talking Heads en route to the dairy-products aisle, we will not find it so hard to accept the ersatz as ultimate authenticity. The point is not roots but connections, the more far-fetched the better. How far from its point of origin can an artifact wash up? How wildly can its original intent be distorted while remaining tantalizingly recognizable? It becomes part of listening to chart the migration of materials, to note, for instance, how the Bacharach-David number "Me Japanese Boy I Love You," a sleekly efficient Orientalist confection originally sung by Bobby Goldsboro in 1964, is eventually woven by the Japanese group the Pizzicato Five into their methodically hip pop-art collages of an imaginary 1960s in which James Bond and Twiggy figure as benign, lighter-than-air demigods. In the world of lounge music, collage is indispensable, if only because there is so much music to be listened to—a whole world of buried recordings—that only by mixing it up as rapidly and heterogeneously as possible can one even begin to sample all the different genres and subgenres.

It was sampling (the extrapolation of fragments of preexisting recordings into repeated figures, or their insertion as isolated sound effects, a practice that has transformed pop music) that was doubtless responsible for the dredging up of much of this material in the first place. That aura of fragmentation—the sense that music can be appreciated just as well out of order, in pieces, juxtaposed inappropriately with other fragments—is perhaps the only atmosphere in which one can sanely approach a potentially infinite canon. Yet the manifest need for editing is balanced against a simmering desire to hear everything, to accept the late-night television offer (featured in one of Robert Klein's comic monologues) of "every record ever made since recording began." Listening to all the records substitutes for leading all the lives, being in all the places. The deliberately all-encompassing category of lounge music signals a relaxation that permits an endless series of brightly lit dream sequences set in imaginary epochs: no identity, no history, no reason to regret anything ever again.

3.

The catch is that, even for someone who was there at the time, the original experience has by now become almost as much a fantasy. The question of what exactly we remember when we listen to old recordings, or whether it can be called remembering at all, becomes less and less answerable over a lifetime. In that commonest of fetishistic practices—the repeated listening to the same song, year after year and decade after decade—does one reenact an original experience, or shut out memory by substituting a fixed pattern of sounds tied to an equally fixed pattern of associations? Can one hope to hear new and different things over the course of time, or would that interfere with the need to be reassured by an unvarying response?

Every listener's personal history can be stitched together from recollections of first encounters, recollections that in due course become private legends. There is some piece of vinyl that is forever March 23, 1962. It is the peculiar faculty of music to make each such first encounter, in retrospect, a snapshot of what the world was at that moment, as if sound were the most absorbent medium of all, soaking up histories and philosophical systems and physical surroundings and encoding them in something so slight as a single vocal quaver or harpsichord interjection. The listener wants not merely to hear the beloved record again, but to hear it always for the first time. The shock of coming up against music that sounds new—whether the encounter is with a Caruso 78 of "Santa Lucia" or the Basie band broadcasting live from the Famous Door or the flip side of the new Zombies single—involves the apprehension, or the invention, of an unsuspected reality, an emotional shade not defined until then, the revelation (tenuous or overpowering) of an alternate future. If music promised anything less than entry into a new world, how account for its hold on the many for whom it can stand in, if need be, for a belief system or a way of life?

In pursuit of an archaeology of memory, it is sometimes possible to reconstruct the encounter: you enter a room just as an unknown song is beginning to play and have an impression that the room changes, the weather of the day is imprinted for future recollection. You had been warned, perhaps: "You've got to hear this one." The song is, for instance, "What the World Needs Now Is Love," a newly released Imperial single by Jackie DeShannon, with words by Hal David and music by Burt Bacharach. It is an April afternoon in 1965, and this year, in the world beyond high school, the usual urgencies of the season seem to converge with a broader impatience in the whole culture, as if things were going to have to move just a little faster to get on with all the necessary impending changes.

The song's impact has a great deal to do with its emphatic deployment of the word "now": the eternal imperatives of lyric warmth are being enlisted into a program of worldwide empathy under the momentary leadership of Jackie DeShannon, whose stunning promotional photograph is a sort of poster for youth itself as imagined in 1965, the perfect Southern California flower girl, with her miniskirt and straight blond hair, radiating sincerity and spontaneity and the dissolution of hidebound social forms. Yet the defiantly fragile sentiment embodied in her singing exists at the center of the most sophisticated imaginable orchestral setting, in a harmonious wedding of feeling and production machinery. No question of counterculture: the culture itself appears to be changing at its core. In the space of under three minutes you construct a story about the way the world is going, even if your outward registration of this experience may be only to venture the knowing opinion that "this record is going to be huge." Every subsequent playback plays back as well a compressed version of the original circumstances; and that was only one such record out of thousands.

The age of recording is necessarily an age of nostalgia—when was the past so hauntingly accessible?—but its bitterest insight is the incapacity of even the most perfectly captured sound to restore the moment of its first inscribing. That world is no longer there—on closer listening, probably never was for longer than the instant during which unfamiliar music ripped open spaces equally and drastically unfamiliar. The listener seeking more such encounters may resort to wide-ranging searches for the unheard, anything from Uzbeki wedding music to unreleased garage bands of southern Wisconsin, anything that might spring the unimaginable surprise. Yet the laboriously sought musical epiphany can never compare to the unsought, even unwanted tune whose ambush is violent and sudden: the song the cab driver was tuned to, the song rumbling from the speaker wedged against the fire-escape railing, the song tingling from the transistor on the beach blanket. To locate those songs again can become, with age, something like a religious quest, as suggested by the frequent use of the phrase "Holy Grail" to describe hard-to-find tracks. The collector is haunted by the knowledge that somewhere on the planet an intact chunk of his past still exists, uncorrupted by time or circumstance.

4.

It was a devotional impulse of sorts that from the outset gave that music such power over its listeners. Where some lit candles, others listened to the Shirelles. To fully reconstruct how one came to be haunted by the memory of endlessly playing both sides of Lou Johnson's 45 of "Kentucky Bluebird" backed with "The Last One To Be Loved" in the fall of 1964, or, a few months earlier (it was the moment when Burt Bacharach's name first meant something), registering the impact of Dionne Warwick singing "Walk On By," it is perhaps necessary to recollect the way the 45-rpm record once provided the basis for something like a religion, or at any rate a religion of art. For a youth culture that had not yet discovered its destiny to change the world, cultural life was often a matter of keeping up with the Top 40 countdown when it was released each Sunday, to culminate in the apotheosis of: "And this week's Hot 100 Billboard number one record is . . . 'Game of Love' by Wayne Fontana and the Mindbenders!" The transistor radio at minimal volume, listened to well after midnight, could seem like a direct line to the Godhead: in the heart of emptiness and darkness, music continued to pour out.

Functionally, the 45 was something of a detour from that forward sweep of technological progress by which the long-playing record had liberated popular music from the temporal constraints of the 78. The LP allowed a symphony to be heard straight through without messing around with three or four fragile shellac discs, and permitted Duke Ellington, for example, to create extended suites; listeners could go about their housework or their homework or their lovemaking for as long as half an hour without having to turn the record over. The 45, by contrast, perpetuated the time limits of the 78, although in an admittedly greatly improved form: miniaturized, lightweight, and unbreakable, it could be held in the palm of the hand yet contained immeasurable depths and reaches, a perfect mystical object made of cheap plastic.

Its virtues were not limited to cheapness. Pop LPs tended to be diffuse affairs in which one or two hits were surrounded by filler of varying quality; the 45 by contrast focused attention unwaveringly on a solitary object of desire. If the B side turned out to be worthy of attention, that was merely a gratuitous extra fillip. (In the faith defined by 45s, the cultivation of brilliant and obscure B-sides represented the occult or esoteric branch.) Listening to a 45 was a separate act, preceded by careful selection and given reverently close attention. Each was judged by how completely and unpredictably it mapped a reality in its allotted playing time: the best seemed to carve vast stretches out of that limited duration, while the worst seemed endless even at a minute and a half.

The density of pop music in the Sixties was such that any week might yield two or three or more of these life-changing experiences, whether emanating from Detroit or London or Memphis or Los Angeles. The impact of the Beatles and the Beach Boys, Motown and Stax-Volt, Curtis Mayfield and James Brown and Aretha Franklin and Bob Dylan, did not register successively but more or less simultaneously. Many scores of secondary figures contributed records equally impressive: Billy Stewart ("Sitting in the Park") or the Castaways ("Liar Liar"), the Left Banke ("Walk Away Renee") or Barbara Lewis ("Hello Stranger") or Fontella Bass ("Rescue Me") would crop up with the unexpected force of a prophetic visitation, explosions of feeling amid a ground bass provided by reliable rhythm machines ranging from "Louie, Louie" to "Boogaloo Down Broadway."

The songs that Burt Bacharach and Hal David were writing in those years were not marginal but central to all that, and it is a little disconcerting to find Bacharach treated after all these years as a quaint anachronism in whom, after all, some remarkable qualities can be found. Bacharach's music became a victim of the Balkanizing tendency of a latter-day pop music industry happiest when "niche-marketing" one subdivision or another of a pop universe that in the mid-1960s was briefly and weirdly convergent.

It made perfect sense for Sam Cooke, a gospel singer metamorphosed into pop idol, to sing Bob Dylan's "Blowin' in the Wind" on his *Live at the Copa* album, for Motown headliner Marvin Gaye to pay album-length tribute to Nat King Cole, for Otis Redding to adapt the Rolling Stones' "Satisfaction," for the Who to record the theme from the TV series *Batman*, for both Bobby Darin and Jim Morrison to sing Kurt Weill, or for the Beatles to record material by the Shirelles, Buck Owens and His Buckaroos, and Buddy Holly, not to mention a song from *The Music Man*. Genre-bending and marketing crossovers were becoming the norm, and the Top 40 sound of any given moment was likely to be a curious amalgam of disparate elements, "Stranger in the Night" followed immediately by "Papa's Got a Brand New Bag," the Troggs in regular rotation with Herb Alpert and the Tijuana Brass. A hit was a hit.

5.

In biographical notes Bacharach tends to sound like the sum of his training and influences: a songwriter who cites both Ravel's *Daphnis and Chloé* and the late Forties work of Charlie Parker and Miles Davis as pivotal in his musical development; who studied with Henry Cowell, Bohuslav Martinu, and Darius Milhaud; and who took his skills into the heart of what was then still a thriving "adult popular" market, as accompanist-arranger for Vic Damone, Polly Bergen, and Steve Lawrence, and as musical director in the late 1950s for Marlene Dietrich's international tours. Yet all that might have counted for nothing had he not collided with the songwriting culture symbolized by the Brill Building at 1619 Broadway, where in the early 1960s hit songs were being concocted with something approaching industrial precision by teams like Carole King and Gerry Goffin, Barry Mann and Cynthia Weil, and Jerry Leiber and Mike Stoller.

Bacharach's earliest hits were very much part of that wider musical scene, and many feel that for melodic invention he never really surpassed early songs like "Any Day Now" or "Make It Easy on Yourself" or "It's Love That Really Counts." Bacharach never evolved into a rock-and-roller (his song for Manfred Mann, "My Little Red Book," is a fascinatingly stylized approximation of rock-and-roll, or perhaps a veiled commentary on its limitations), but pop music as defined in the Brill Building (and its Southern California equivalents) still had plenty of room for records that were neither dance music nor exclusively youth music. It is impossible to imagine how Bacharach's art might have evolved had he not had the good fortune to connect with the emotional directness of ballads like Jerry Leiber and Phil Spector's "Spanish Harlem" and King and Goffin's "Oh No, Not My Baby." In his later songs he seems torn between an almost disdainfully virtuosic elaborateness (the relatively unpopular masterpiece "Looking with My Eyes") and a knowing command of the simplistic (the hugely successful jingle "Raindrops Keep Fallin' on My Head"); the earlier compositions suggest no such conflict.

The Rhino box set—well selected and densely and usefully annotated—turns out to be something of a eulogy for an era that can be characterized simply by citing some of the artists, familiar or mostly forgotten, for whom Bacharach and David tailored their songs: Chuck Jackson, Gene Pitney, the Shirelles, Jerry Butler, Bobby Vinton, Brook Benton, Jack Jones, and of course Dionne Warwick, who first showed up as part of a trio of backup singers and went on to record over sixty Bacharach-David songs. (It would be a significant event if only for making available four of the singer Lou Johnson's great and weirdly unsuccessful first recordings of some of Bacharach's best songs, most notably "The Last One to Be Loved.")

Later would come the British contingent (not all represented here)—Tom Jones, Cilla Black, the Walker Brothers, and the sublime Dusty Springfield—to fill out the picture of a music industry still functioning something like the old Hollywood, obeying notions of classic songwriting form and respecting a sharp division of labor between singers and songwriters, with the indispensable "A&R" (artists and repertoire) men working out the mystical equations to determine who should sing what. It was a world that became more intensely interesting just as it was being hit with the external convulsions that would compel it to ditch much of the old-timers' wisdom and radically regroup.

What finally had to be ditched was the idea of music made, by definition, by professionals, studio guys, real pros with not a trace of amateurism even if they sometimes had to put up with clearly amateurish front-liners that the kids went for. The music's identifying mark was a combination of perfectionism and commercialism, both unquestioned: not just slick sounds and the finest engineering, but the real poetry that could sense the underground current that made all the difference between Top 40 and nothing.

The records bore wherever necessary the reassuring touch of the studio professional who could do anything on demand: cowboys and Indians, dawn in the tropics, sea chanty, snake charmer oboe solo, doo-wop under the overpass. A single chord, a single smear or deftly warped echo could put you at the county fair or in lover's lane or on the fringes of the Outer Limits. The idea was to make the perfect record—perfection being certified by grosses—and admiration for the calculation and control that went into it was part of the listener's response as well. The ultimate miracles of expression could not be planned, of course, but they sounded a lot better when all that backup was in place.

Fans listened to the new releases as if they were assessing new machines, checking out how smoothly the gears worked and what effect they produced from different angles, in different settings. Every element was up for examination: how the singing compared with the competition, the lyrics of the second verse, the peculiar organ break, the breathless spoken interjection toward the end. There was no assumption—as there would be in the wake of hits like the Kingsmen's "Louie Louie"—that the listeners could produce such a record themselves. It really was like the movies, with a wide screen and a cast of thousands: a superb technical feat created solely for the pleasure of the fans, as they could verify if they cared to by reading the copy in magazines like *Hit Parader* and *Song Hits*, or by sampling liner notes that tended to posit a relentlessly productive show business, driven by nothing more than the optimistic energies of seasoned veterans and youthful go-getters.

What no one who cared ever doubted was that they were in the presence, often enough, of deliberate beauty; there were no accidents here. Least of all in the Bacharach records (not originally billed as such, but increasingly recognizable) which had no need for echo effects or other electronic distortion to make their point. The musical elements were clearly exposed, so that even the most casual listener would notice how every note contributed. These were total compositions, to be appreciated like a series of paintings: "Baby It's You" (its spareness allowing abysses to open between its lines, the "sha la la" chorus washing mournfully like chill surf over rock) or "Any Day Now" (the limits of its landscape of feeling laid out almost sternly by strings, organ, and drums, leaving the words—"then the blue shadows will fall all over town"—free to go about their work of suggestion). If many pop records (Phil Spector's, for instance) sought to recede into a curtain of indeterminate sound, the Bacharach songs were placed against a backdrop of silence: everything of which the record consisted was audible and distinguishable. The little cowboy symphony "The Man Who Shot Liberty Valance" (with Gene Pitney singing Hal David's deft synopsis of the John Ford movie) seemed, right from its annunciatory fiddle line, a synthesis of songs that were already synthetic, even farther from any conceivable prairie than the Hollywood themes of Dimitri Tiomkin and Elmer Bernstein and Jerome Moross: a pocket West, scrimshawed into two and a half minutes.

Bacharach, by his own account, "was thinking in terms of miniature movies . . . with peak moments and not one intensity level the whole way through. . . . You can tell a story and be able to be explosive one minute, then get quiet as kind of a satisfying resolution." In these movies the singer was only one of the actors, enacting a drama in which the instruments had just as integral a part to play; the hooks, those key phrases with which a record has to make itself memorable to the one-time listener, were as likely to be played as sung. Here there was no such thing as background; every sound participated in articulating the narrative.

6.

When people talk about Bacharach they generally have in mind his intersection with the lyrics of Hal David and the singing of Dionne Warwick. The three produced a body of work whose richness is barely sketched by the Rhino box set; Warwick's early albums consist of almost nothing but Bacharach-David songs, all of them interesting to listen to and many still not widely known. What the three apparently shared, aside from anything else, was a relishing of difficulty, whether of pitch or meter or rhyme or narrative compression; their records make no appeal to special effects or topical allusions. Bacharach would come to be identified almost exclusively with the products of this three-way collaboration, whose dissolution brought to an end his long run of extraordinary productivity.

By the same token, the associations called up by Bacharach's music become inextricably entangled with David's peculiar blend of sophisticated versification and heartfelt emotional statement, a blend in which the encroachments of the maudlin are generally kept at bay by the dexterity of rhymes, the syntactical clarity that anchors Bacharach's profuse melody lines, and the elliptical elegance of his storytelling. The bridge from "Do You Know the Way to San Jose," overfamiliar though it may be, is a striking demonstration of his skill:

L. A. is a great big freeway,
Put a hundred down and buy a car;
In a week, maybe two, they'll make you a star.

Weeks turn into years, how quick they pass,
And all the stars that never were
Are parking cars and pumping gas.

It is impossible to measure how much Warwick adds to the tone of the songs, since so many of them were written for the benefit of her interpretation. The persona created by her vocal art reveals her to be as much actor as singer; and around her laconic pleadings, interrupted gasps, and almost successfully suppressed cries of anger an implied dramatic universe begins to form.

By borrowing stray elements from the surrounding air, the listener could fill in the implications of these arias without operas. Here was adult romance, born under the same astrological signs that presided over *Sex and the Single Girl* (book and movie) and the novels of Jacqueline Susann (in one of them the characters even talk about Bacharach), the Pill, and the perfume ads that instructed: "Want him to be more of a man? Try being more of a woman." The romantic dreamworld of Manhattan rain covering up tears on the mascara cohabited uneasily with the leering ambience of Sixties sex comedies—old men's movies, born antiquated—like *Who's Been Sleeping in My Bed* and *Sunday in New York*, movies that seemed to emanate from the Esquire cartoon world of goggle-eyed, overweight execs chasing voluptuously stacked secretaries around the desk in private offices; movies like *Made in Paris* and *Promise Her Anything* and *Wives and Lovers*, remembered now mostly because Burt Bacharach wrote tie-in songs for them.

Hal David's lyrics lightly sketched in a world of rainy days and breakups and telephones, airports and doorbells, makeup and taxis, "an empty tube of toothpaste and a half-filled cup of coffee": and, unmentioned, booze and Valium and cigarettes, therapists and exercise programs, broken glass, hours of silence and immobility, crowded bars and dates gone sour: a woman's world, most of the time, the world as it might be imagined by the one who didn't go to the disco, who stayed home watching some old Olivia de Havilland movie—the one with the nice girl undermined and nearly destroyed by her murderous schizophrenic sister, perhaps—and who would despite all be obliged to show up Monday morning and somehow shuffle through the monthly billing. Billy Wilder's movie *The Apartment*, with its themes of wage slavery and sexual harassment, was the perfect source material for Bacharach and David's only Broadway musical, *Promises, Promises*.

In the heart of the record was a cry from inside a box. A song like "In Between the Heartaches" evokes a hidden universe of pain, a love song for a distant or abusive lover sometimes kind enough to make things nice for a while. But the crackups are private, under control as long as anyone is watching: this is a well-bred melancholia, the hidden side of a Kennedy-era effervescence personified outwardly by Burt himself, casual in knit turtleneck and loafers, flanked by his glamorous wife Angie Dickinson and his close associates Marlene Dietrich and Dionne Warwick, the inhabitants of a world where nothing is likely to go seriously wrong.

Kennedy died in November 1963, but songs like "A House Is Not a Home" and "Wives and Lovers" and "Land of Make Believe" just kept on coming: future souvenirs of the awareness that once upon a time one was fooled by appearances, got conned for a moment by the delusions of glamour and celebrity, actually believed that the people in those photographs were having fun. The disco scene in *What's New Pussycat?*, with Peter O'Toole and Romy Schneider frugging insouciantly under red lights to the music of Manfred Mann, incarnated with appropriate randomness the frothy evanescence of a scene already over by the time any public ever caught its afterglimmer. The Kennedy Sixties could be like that, were like that for most of the audience: a succession of parties that one hadn't attended, leaving in their wake, through the medium of film clips and candid shots and songs, a detritus of feathers and glitter.

As the decade moved forward or downward, these ballads inevitably became emblems of the part of the Sixties that was not about youth, of those listeners who still aspired toward some kind of sleek adulthood, modern and liberated but never sloppy; who coveted nice suits, hairdos with architectonic grace rather than the free flow of the "natural," all the artifices of comfort, the rituals of air travel, whatever evoked the big dream of the modern, as if the twentieth century were a reverie best indulged "while you're lounging in your leather chair." (The words are from a song, "Paper Maché," whose satirical commentary on the materialism of consumer culture was far too gracefully muted even to register in the atmosphere of 1970.)

It might be an unreal world but the cravings that defined it would keep coming back, like one of those hooks to which Bacharach's songs were finally reduced in memory; the fragments of tunes rise to the surface at three in the morning, the hour when melodic progression can become a torture implement. Somehow the tunes began to pall; the mood was perhaps a little too upbeat to believe, the charts too anxiously busy; the Seventies had arrived, and it no longer seemed at all likely that the music business would change the world. Unfairly, the Bacharach songs would be perceived to melt into that larger repertoire of sweetened, plaintive, self-pitying ballads to which for the better part of a decade office workers were condemned to listen for eight hours at a stretch. They appeared to be songs for a world that had turned out not to exist.

7.

It's hard not to wonder what sort of songs Bacharach might have written with a different collaborator than Hal David. (Bertolt Brecht, perhaps: think what *Promises, Promises* could have been with its full cynical potential realized.) But in some sense the lyrics hardly mattered to Bacharach's music; he could adapt to anything. All those love scenarios, were they anything more than an occasion to let him play with shapes, textures, pauses, intervals, varieties of harmonic spaces? The tension that singled out Bacharach's songs from the goop in which they sometimes threatened to dissolve came from the sense of a detached intelligence working not against the mood of the songs but outside it.

These intricate compositions are about their own virtuosity, a virtuosity that delights in difficulty and intricacy, and delights even more in disguising them as just another pop tune. At his most characteristic Bacharach exudes a dry constructivist energy: a given song might evoke Stravinsky's *Agon* gone pop, or a fragment of Schönberg deftly sweetened and cajoled, in extremis, back into conventional harmonic resolution. The drama—or the game—of a Bacharach melody is the risk that it might not circle back acceptably, might simply extend outward in a series of increasingly far-flung spirals. How far can he swim from shore before losing all hope of getting back? The melody branches at angles so abrupt that it threatens unbridgeable gaps, unacceptable dissonances: until, with the aplomb of Douglas Fairbanks as Zorro, Bacharach abruptly brings it home by one deft shortcut or another. One can imagine him as a connoisseur of emotional precision, whose own feelings would be irrelevant, the embodiment of a dandyism capable all the same of appreciating the expression of true feeling. In that light the music would be all surface, but the most beautiful surface imaginable.

There was always a temptation to remove the words from the songs, remove any layers of the arrangement that were mere ornamentation, the sonic furniture enabling them to "pass" as acceptable AM product. Set free from their context and commercial purpose—no longer in the business of selling a particular three-minute emotional drama—those changes and textures could then be reassembled as parts of some symphonic suite, the sort of extended composition that Bacharach evidently had no interest in pursuing. The nostalgia that is so often the theme of Hal David's lyrics might suggest by extension the listener's inchoate yearning for another song hidden within the actual song, a wild kernel of shape-making.

In the early soundtracks *What's New Pussycat?*, *After the Fox*, and *Casino Royale*, a hidden aspect of Bacharach's talent emerges: not the romantic whole-heartedness one might have expected from a composer known for his love songs, but rather a parodistic collage of styles, the Charleston rearranged for harpsichord, a Neapolitan street song metamorphosing into strip-joint fanfare and again into a pastiche of *L'Histoire du Soldat*. "Here I Am" and "The Look of Love" are employed in comic movie settings calculated to undercut the effect of two of Bacharach's most beautiful ballads. Nobody will notice, it's only a silly movie, so he can play games with structure and instrumentation and mood, games that predict a good many more solemn exercises in postmodern patchwork.

By reinterpretation musicians might of course try to tease out those unsounded implications, yet Bacharach's songs prove curiously recalcitrant to improvisers; they were designed to work roughly the same way no matter who sings or plays them. Whether by Cilla Black, Dionne Warwick, the Delfonics, or Stevie Wonder, "Alfie" stubbornly remains "Alfie." The televised tribute "One Amazing Night" ended up sounding more like Karaoke Night, so little did the younger performers add to earlier versions of Bacharach-David standards. As a vehicle for jazz musicians, Bacharach's music seems too tightly constructed to permit much fruitful alteration; Sonny Rollins chose wisely to play "A House Is Not a Home" pretty much note for note.

In jazz albums devoted to Bacharach tunes, the jazz component tends to be more or less tacked on to songs that stubbornly resist being bent out of shape. When the concept works, as on Stan Getz's 1968 album *What the World Needs Now*, it's because Getz contents himself with virtually singing the songs on sax, while McCoy Tyner's elaborations on the similarly titled 1996 outing *What the World Needs Now: The Music of Burt Bacharach* seem superfluous ornamentations of tunes that come pre-ornamented. (A more interesting approach was taken by Walter Becker and Donald Fagen in their composition "Rapunzel," a bop tune based on the chords of "Land of Make Believe"[4]: here the hooklike aspects of Bacharach's writing are undercut, the melody made essentially unrecognizable so that its inner structure can be turned inside out.)

Of all the recent variations, John Zorn's *Great Jewish Music: Burt Bacharach* collection is finally the

---

4. It is performed by the Pete Christlieb–Warne Marsh Quintet on their 1978 album *Apogee.*

most satisfying and, oddly, the most faithful. It lends credence to the notion that the way to recapture the past is to tear it apart. At its best it is something like the Burt Bacharach album of one's dreams: not adding further decoration to the tunes, but stripping away textures and trappings to find the song's skeleton. Bacharach lends himself to austere treatments because what counts in his music is fundamentally austere. The hard core of that music has always been curiously at odds with his image as diffident aristocrat given to breeding race horses, or strolling along that pristine stretch of Southern California beachfront that one imagines as his natural habitat. The period colorings of nostalgia, the mythology that would make him a kind of walking advertisement for the Good Life, are finally irrelevant; he is a maker of patterns whose stark durable structures can give endless pleasure without having to be about something, as if to confirm Stravinsky's dictum that "music itself does not signify anything."[5]

---

5. In *Stravinsky in Conversation with Robert Craft* (Doubleday, 1959).

ABOUT THE TYPE

The text type, Sabon, was designed by the son of a letter-painter, Jan Tschichold (1902–1974), who was jointly commissioned in 1960 by Monotype, Linotype, and Stempel to create a typeface that would produce consistent results when produced by hand-setting, or with either the Monotype or Linotype machines.

The German book designer and typographer is known for producing a wide range of designs. Tschichold's early work, considered to have revolutionized modern typography, was influenced by the avant-garde Bauhaus and characterized by bold asymmetrical sans serif faces. With his Sabon design, Tschichold demonstrates his later return to more formal and traditional typography. Sabon is based upon the roman Garamond face of Konrad Berner, who married the widow of printer Jacques Sabon. The italic Sabon is modeled after the work of Garamond contemporary, Robert Granjon.

In Sabon, Tschichold's appreciation of classical letters melds with the practicality of consistency and readability into a sophisticated and adaptable typeface.

Printed and bound by R. R. Donnelley & Sons,
Harrisonburg, Virginia